SO-CAA-513

K. R. CONWAY

CRUEL SUMMER

To Kat —
Always be brave.
KR Cy

Wicked Whale
Publishing

This book is a work of fiction. Names, characters, and incidents are the product of the author's imagination or are used fictitiously. Any resemblance to actual events, locales, or persons living or dead, is coincidental.

First Edition: March 2015

Cover Design: Cape Cod Scribe
Editor: Charlotte C. Breslin, Skeleton Key Editing

Copyright © 2015 by Kathleen R. Conway All rights reserved. In accordance with U.S. Copyright Act of 1976, the scanning, uploading and electronic sharing of any part of this book without the permission of the publisher / author is unlawful piracy and theft of the author's intellectual property. If you would like to use material from this book (other than for review purposes), prior written permission must be obtained by contacting the publisher at wickedwhalepublishing.com. Thank you for your support of the author's rights.

Library of Congress Cataloging-in-Publication Data
Conway, Kathleen R.
Cruel Summer/ by Kathleen R. Conway – First Edition.
    Pages: 342
    Summary: When an immortal killer finds himself stranded on Cape Cod at the height of the Fourth of July week with a stolen car and a body in the trunk, he is forced to accept the help of an outspoken female mechanic, who changes his outlook on life, love, and monsters.

Wicked Whale Publishing
Bourne MA 02532
www.WickedWhalePublishing.com

ISBN: 978-0-9897763-6-3

Published in the United States of America

~ DEDICATION ~

For the fans, because they rock my world!

And for Uncle Phil, because he would've loved *Cerberus* more

than anybody . . .

Dear Reader:

This story is a prequel novel regarding the characters Kian, Ana, and MJ. In the timeframe of the series, this book takes place before the first book, UNDERTOW.

While Cruel Summer can be read at any point in the series, it DOES contain some story spoilers for UNDERTOW. Therefore, if you are someone who likes surprises, it is highly recommended that you read UNDERTOW first.

Then again, you may be like me and try to peek inside the gifts way before you are supposed to open them . . .

Read at your own risk and ENJOY!

K. R. CONWAY

CRUEL SUMMER

~ PART 1 ~
LIES

1

KIAN

THE 1935 AUBURN SPEEDSTER was easily the finest automobile I had ever driven in my 182 years. With its curving lines, huge fenders, and miles of chrome, it was the pinnacle of vehicular perfection.

Unfortunately the car's former owner, whose body was wedged in the trunk, was really ruining my evening at this point.

Granted, Samuel Benton, who barely fit in the Auburn's tight cargo area, had been a greasy weasel of a man with a severely overinflated ego. At only five and a half feet tall, he had reminded me of one of those monkeys from the circus that bounce around at the end of a rope, clamoring for a bit of attention. Thanks to his thriving cocaine business, he had thought of himself as a god, which made him even more irritating.

Luckily his stellar personality made killing him an hour ago quite enjoyable, and I took my time dragging every ounce of life-force from his ratty little body, like a smoker enjoying a fine cigar.

He thought I'd come for a hit of his over-priced powder.

He didn't realize that *he* was my drug of choice.

Honestly, I never would've come to his vacation villa on the Cape, except that he had the one thing I really wanted – his car. The fact that he happened to be at home when I arrived was simply a perk. Dinner on the go, as it were.

The Auburn was everything I'd been searching for in a new toy, and had glided down the street towards the harbor like a bead of liquid mercury. That is, until it mutinied just before 11pm, sputtering to a halt and stranding me in a darkened, dirt-covered parking lot with Sam. He was destined to smell up my new ride if I didn't ditch his body soon.

I thrummed my fingers over the leather steering wheel, staring through the night at the side of some run down building named The Milk Way, which I could've sworn was a blacksmith's place a few decades ago.

I knew where I was, and breaking down in this exact location, a few hundred yards from Elizabeth Walker's house, had to be some sort of cosmic penance for stealing Benton's car.

Not for killing Benton, however.

That twit deserved what he got.

I watched as a lanky boy in an apron walked along the side of the building, carrying trash bags to the dumpsters for the third time. He was humming to himself, totally oblivious to my presence . . . and how rotten his job was, apparently. He hadn't seen me roll silently into the far end of the parking lot, which probably was a good thing since Benton was with me.

Well, technically his body was with me.

After I'd drained him of his life force, I shot him up with enough cocaine to take out an elephant. I had intended to drive his slowly stiffening carcass to the harbor and dump him in the water, where the cops would think he had overdosed. But no – instead I was stuck with a half-million dollar car that wouldn't start and a dead drug dealer in the trunk.

To make matters far worse, it was Thursday night and the coming week was the start of the July 4th holiday, which meant that every loser in New England would head to the Cape. And being that it was 11pm, no bloody garage would be open to check what the hell was wrong with the Auburn.

God, I hated Cape Cod.

At this point, with karma kicking my ass, I didn't even care that the area was a prime hunting ground thanks to all the swimmers. Stealing souls from beach-goers was like taking candy from snot-nosed brats, thus making the Cape a great place for my kind to kick back and soak up a few souls.

We Mortis made tourist season quite the killer.

Killing swimmers was an art of which I was well practiced. Like my fellow soul sharks, I could hold my breath for hours, staying submerged within the valleys between the sandbars, waiting for a human to cross the dark channel of water. Shadows would cling to me like a velvet skin when I needed them to, making nighttime the best time to hunt. I usually kept tabs on bonfire parties and the occasional group of night surfers since they were the optimal targets; drunken and therefore fairly stupid.

Of course, the real trick to making murder look like an accident was to draw from the swimmers slowly, weakening them so they couldn't fight their way to the sanctuary of the ocean's surface. As they panicked and weakened, they would begin to suck water into their lungs.

That was the key - water in the lungs.

Young soul sharks tended to get too overzealous and not allow their target to draw in water. No water in the lungs equaled no report of drowning from the coroner's office.

Morons.

Despite the wealth of targets on the Cape at the moment, I only wanted one thing: to escape this godforsaken town as soon as possible.

If I was lucky, the kid in the apron would go about his menial job and close up the shack he worked at, never the wiser that I was camped out in the far corner of the parking lot.

True, I'd be stuck here until the town fell silent, but then I could hopefully hike my way to nearby Craigville beach and dump Benton without being noticed. Then, tomorrow morning, I could deal with the car.

As I ran every conceivable way to move a murder victim to a dump site without being caught, I heard the kid's phone ring. I glanced up, half bored, half pissed I wasn't halfway to New York by now, and focused on the thin cell phone the kid brought to his ear.

Even from a distance, I could easily hear him answer the phone, thanks to my advanced eavesdropping ability.

God, I loved the perks of being me.

"There you go. Calling me when I'm super busy, breaking my flow. Sheesh — you're such a bad influence!" scolded the kid with a laugh, leaning back against a large outdoor freezer. He picked at a frazzled thread on his faded apron and his lips twisted into a grin as he listened to the caller. I was about to tune out his teenaged stupidity until I saw his smile fall sharply and his face grow serious.

"Then don't go home. Swing in here — you can crash at my place. No. NO. It's fine — my mom won't care. No, she won't. SHE WON'T! Listen to . . . yeah, I know, but you know you should wait."

The kid had gone from easy going to strung-out stressed in a matter of seconds. Morbid curiosity (and an obscene amount of boredom) made me continue to listen in.

The kid began pacing, and then suddenly turned, heading in my direction.

Concerned that he had seen me, I immediately began trying to figure out where I could stash HIS body if need be. While I loved the Auburn, the lack of storage was going to be a problem at this rate.

Thankfully the kid turned, heading toward a black Wrangler that was parked closer to the road. He yanked open the door, still arguing with the caller as he leaned in to get something.

"You know damn well that I'm right. Just come here and at least hang out. What do ya mean, why? Stop being such a pain in my ass, and just come over. Not to mention I've got something to show you."

I saw the kid slap his hand to his forehead and mouth a few silent curses. He obviously didn't have anything to show this person. Talk about a poorly planned lie.

Idiot.

But then he began looking around the area near the shop, obviously trying to think up SOMETHING to show the stubborn jerk on the other end of the phone, and his eyes landed on my mostly hidden car.

Crap.

I really needed more trunk space. If his stupid friend shows up, I may need to carjack a bloody minivan.

The kid squinted in my direction, trying to make out the lines of Benton's former vehicle.

I needed a plan, fast. I drew a deep breath as I heard the kid tell the caller that there was some *"sick looking ride"* sitting in the corner of the parking lot. I watched him begin to approach my car, and rather than stay behind the wheel like a psycho-stalker, I decided to confront the kid.

Then kill him if he didn't leave me alone.

As I pushed open the heavy door, I heard the kid say to the caller that I might be broken down. *"Jeez, he's not a serial killer! Chill out! I'm just going to go knock — oh, hang on. He's getting out."*

He turned his attention away from his phone as he approached. "Hey man – nice ride. You having car trouble?" he asked.

I cleared my throat and began lying, "It stalled out on me, but it's not a big deal. I have a friend coming in a while to help me out." Hopefully this kid would move along with his insignificant life still intact.

"Well, I know a great mechanic. I'm on the phone with her right now," chirped the kid.

I couldn't help but laugh. "A girl? Your mechanic is a chick? Yeah – that's okay, but I think I'll pass. Wouldn't want her to chip a nail on my engine or something. I'll just wait for my friend, but thanks."

A girl. How ridiculous.

I thought the kid would take a hint and leave, but instead a smirk climbed up his face as he brought the phone slowly back to his mouth. "Yeah, he's broken down, but he says not to worry about looking at the car. He said he wouldn't want you to break a nail."

I heard a sharp voice say something loudly in reply through the phone, and the kid winced, pulling it away from his ear so he wouldn't have hearing damage. When the line went quiet, he carefully brought the phone back to his cheek. "Hello?" he asked, but the caller had apparently hung up.

He stuffed his phone into the front pocket of his apron and reached his hand out to shake. "She'll be here in just a second. I'm MJ, by the way."

"Terrific," I replied sarcastically. I took his hand, giving it a firm shake as I began to wish I had a fucking mommy mobile. "I'm Kian. Kian O'Reilly."

I wanted to strangle someone . . . anyone.

Even a dog would do.

2

 KIAN

IT TOOK MSS PISSED about ten minutes to get to the shop, though trying to maintain small talk with the walking apron was a new level of hell for me. He went on and on about bands I'd never heard of, ice cream flavors that I'd never taste, and the infinite joys of living by the beach.

When he rolled into a monologue about how *totally wicked* the surfing at Cahoon's Hollow was, I nearly thought about killing myself. Nearly.

But then I pictured backing the Auburn over him as soon as it was running, and felt instantly better.

As he began describing the new graphics he was getting added to his board, a beaten-up four door roared into the parking lot, sending dust and dirt scattering.

"Oh good! She's here! She's amazing with cars!" proclaimed the kid who had turned his attention to the new arrival, whose vehicle seemed to yack up a piston as it sputtered and died.

In the momentary silence, I could hear the bass beat of the radio playing inside the car. I braced myself as the door began to open, sure I was going to be hit with 100 decibels of angry chick rock. Instead, it was Green Day who blared through the empty parking lot.

Okay – so she had good taste in music. That didn't mean she could identify a screwdriver.

I watched as a riot of black hair twined with purple streaks appeared from the door, quickly followed by a faded green tank top and grease-covered cargo pants encasing an entirely feminine frame. As she turned I finally got to see her huge, blue eyes lined with black eyeliner, and lush pink lips that seemed to sparkle in the street lamp's light. She looked me over, crossing her arms fiercely over her chest, effectively enhancing her delicate cleavage and ramping up her mean-girl attitude to a stellar level of sexiness.

I let my eyes drift over her, taking in the barely-there curve of her body, the graceful arch of her shoulders, and the rope bracelet that hugged her sun-kissed skin. A golden belly-button ring winked at me from her navel as she tossed her hip to the side, leaning against the car she rode in on.

She was Tinker Bell's bad-ass, smoking hot, alter-ego. And granted, she was technically a walking meal ticket to me, but *damn*. For a moment I thought that humans might actually carry more potential than simply snack-value.

But then I dragged my gaze back up to her face and all lustfulness that I'd been entertaining, shriveled.

The look she was giving me could crack a windshield.

11

I straightened and began to approach her, but she shoved off her car as Apron Boy tried to introduce me to her. She ignored him and walked right past me, headed for the Auburn.

She stopped at the front of the massive car and began running her fingers under the lip of the side hood, searching for the latch. As she did so, she glared at me. "So – what did ya do? Raid the museum?"

Raid the what?

"Hey – Kennedy. I asked you a question. Where'd ya get this thing?" she demanded again, jutting her chin toward the Auburn as the hood finally gave a *click*, releasing.

She began to lift the massive slab of steel and I snapped out of my momentary confusion. "Here – I got that," I said coming to her aid.

"I don't need your help. Me and my *delicate* fingernails are just fine without your over-dressed muscles."

As if to prove her point, she raised the huge hood above her five-foot tall frame, pulling up the hood stand to prop it open. As she stretched on her tip-toes, the top rode even higher . . . and those damn cargo shorts slid dangerously low on her lean hips.

"HEY – eyes up here," she scolded sharply, pointing to her face.

I couldn't help a devilish smirk.

The girl had sass. I could get down with that.

She glared at me. "You gonna screw your head on straight and tell me where you got a '35 Auburn, or just stand there like an overpriced lawn ornament?"

"Excuse me?" I demanded. Suddenly sass wasn't so appealing. "Who do you think you are, talking to someone you don't know like that?"

"I'm the person who is gonna save your khaki-clad ass from the side of the road, so you can hurry off to the next ocean-front orgy and show off your metal man parts to all the ladies," she replied, gesturing to the Auburn. "Men that drive cars like this are trying to make up for certain shortcomings, if ya know what I mean," she winked.

"I assure you that nothing of mine is short," I muttered under my breath. One part of me wanted to snap her neck, but the other part was totally intrigued.

She was unlike anyone I'd ever met – prickly, intelligent, and twistedly addictive in a tooth-fairy-gone-wrong sort of way. Sadly, I was fairly sure she'd rather remove my maleness than ever let me get near her, so I decided to do the next best thing: piss her off.

I took a step towards her as she looked over the engine. "First of all, how I got the car is not your business. Secondly, we are not on the side of the road, Pixie Pants. We're in a parking lot, and a shitty one at that. You should be more observant of your surroundings."

"HEY! Our parking lot is not shitty!" protested the apron, who had wandered back towards the ice cream shop. Or rather, shack. He watched me and Pix from afar, probably to make sure I wasn't a creeper, though the mini-mechanic appeared to be feisty enough to hold her own.

"So what's the verdict, Pixie Pants?" I asked with a wide grin.

She didn't look up, but continued to fiddle with the engine, checking fluids. "Call me Pixie Pants again and I'll make sure your ride turns into a fireball before you make it past the harbor."

"You're so delightful – like a scorpion on acid. Did anyone ever tell you that?" I purred, taking another step closer, pretending to be interested in how her fingers traced over the mechanics of my car as she bent over the engine.

"My stellar personality wins me the popular vote all the time." She stood back, wiping the grease from her fingers along the butt of her pants. The lines streaked her rear like a tiger's stripes. I could examine those stripes all day.

She finally turned to look at me, "Try cranking it over now, Kennedy."

"It's Kian," I replied, sliding in behind the wheel.

"Whatever, Daddy Warbucks," she muttered to herself, though I could hear her clearly.

I turned the key and the Auburn shocked me by roaring to life. I couldn't believe she actually fixed it. The sound of the engine purring reminded me why I was so desperate to get the sucker running in the first place.

I still had a corpse to dump.

I left the Auburn running and walked around to the hood. Pixie Pants stood watching god-knows-what-parts in the engine, as if daring them to break down again. I was still amazed she had done it.

"How old are you?" I asked, floored at her ability.

She squeezed by me to reach the hood stand. "Why? Trying to add 'pedophile' and 'pervert' to your long list of charming qualities?"

Ouch.

"Okay, first of all, I'm twenty, not some elderly grandpa looking for a few thrills from a fourteen-year-old." Well . . . technically I was more than 160 years old, but I looked 20. *Pfft – details.*

She shot me a snarky look. "I'm sixteen, almost seventeen, but thanks for labeling me a middle-schooler."

"Hey – you made me guess. Totally your fault. And speaking of the Blame Game, who can I thank for that lovely man-hating vibe you so eloquently give off like shrapnel? An ex-boyfriend who jumped your candy-striper cousin perhaps?"

Her mouth dropped open as she was about to hurl some well-constructed insult my way, but the hood slipped. She moved fast, trying to get out of the way so as not to be decapitated, but in her rush she tripped on her own black boots.

I grabbed her around the waist before she smashed face-first into the gravel.

Immediately she scrambled out of my hold and I could hear her heart rate going far faster than before. She stood there, looking at me, eyes wide, but then she managed to pull herself back into that snarky shell of armor she wore so well.

Her reaction to my touch screamed one thing loud and clear: fear. In that one moment, she was terrified, and not from nearly losing her head.

No. She had been afraid of me.

"You okay?" I asked, stepping back as unease crawled over my skin. She couldn't know what I was – there was no way. Humans couldn't identify what we truly were, which was why we were such effective killers.

Pixie's reaction to my touch, however, was entirely different from that of other humans I'd come in contact with.

"Of course," she snapped, twisting her multicolored hair over one shoulder. She nodded to the Auburn, "You're good to go. I just tweaked the timing."

I nodded, fishing a few hundred dollars from my back pocket. I knew I was overpaying for her work, but between her faded clothing and rust-bucket-on-wheels, I knew she could use the cash.

Plus, I was still running over the look on her face when I had grabbed her. It was haunting. Disturbing.

I took a step towards her, holding out the cash. "Thanks."

She eyed the money, but shook her head. "A twenty is fine. It only took me a few minutes."

Wow. I never knew a human to turn down an easy four hundred dollars. She was like a mini Goth girl with a conscience.

"Just take it – twenty for the car and the other 380 for putting up with me," I urged, smiling.

She rolled her eyes. "Fine. Forty then. I'm not taking more than that. I didn't earn it, despite your breathtaking banter."

"Did you just admit that my banter is breathtaking?" I replied, unable to keep from teasing her.

Her eyes lit with fire. "Are you freakin' kidding me? You know what? Just forget it. I don't need your money." She began stomping off towards her car, muttering things about me and every other spoiled rich washashore that she dealt with each summer.

It was only then that I realized I actually enjoyed her company.

Dear god, I needed to get out of this place.

It was messing with my mind.

Tweaked by my reaction to the whole debacle, I shook my head and trotted after her just as she slid into her car. Apron Boy also ran up to her, and I slowed so he could talk to her without me hovering, though I was close enough to see that she had a few pillows and blankets in the back of her car.

Jeezus, was she sleeping in that rust bucket?

"You're not going home, right?" asked the boy, concern etched over his face.

Pixie sighed, "No, I'm not, so calm down. The Howlers are out tonight, so I'm just going to go hang with them. I can crash at the overlook. You wanna come?"

The boy looked torn and seemed to know who these *Howlers* were. "Shit, I'd love to, but I've got to open tomorrow at the crack of dawn to make a double batch of just about everything. This week is huge for us. I'm sorry, but I can't. My mom would kill me."

"No worries, MJ. I'll text ya later," said Pixie, starting her car. Apron Boy (whose name I'd entirely forgotten was *MJ* until Pixie had reminded me), backed away and I stepped quickly up to her window, propelled by a need that I bloody well didn't understand.

She looked at me and moaned, "Now what?"

Hell if I know.

"I'm paying you. You did a great job and, all joking aside, you deserve the money. So here - take it." I held out the forty dollars she'd agreed to, but as she took it, I let the rest of the cash carefully slip onto the floor behind her seat.

By the time she'd find it, I'd be long gone from the Cape and she'd be forced to keep it. And then, finally – *hopefully* – I could get my screwed up emotions in check.

She looked down at the money in her hand and then up to me. Her eyes were the most stunning, liquid blue I'd ever seen. "You really need to find a mechanic that can handle that Auburn engine. I'd locate one fairly soon."

"I will and thanks again, uh . . . what's your name anyway?" I asked, stepping away from her car as she shifted into drive.

"I'm Ana. Ana Lane," she replied, giving me a quick nod as she pulled out of the parking lot, leaving a trail of dirt in her wake.

I turned to MJ, who was watching her drive away. "So who are the Howlers anyway?" I asked, my curiosity bordering on obsession.

I really needed to get the hell out of here . . .

"That's what the members of the night surfing club call themselves – you know, like they howl at the moon because they know they can go surfing and see well during the full moon. I know – it's a stupid name but it's loads of fun."

"She's going surfing? Right now? IN THE DARK?" Tension ran through me as I knew it was the perfect time to hunt, especially if you were a soul shark, like me.

She'd be a prime target tonight.

Why, *WHY* did I ever come back to the Cape? Benton's car was not worth this amount of bullshit. Nothing good ever happens to me in the Sand Flea state, I swear.

MJ looked at me oddly. "Dude – don't worry. Ana can haul ass on the water. The girl is half sea witch. Not to mention, Marconi beach is really open. The Howlers go there to surf because there aren't any granite rocks to smash your head on. She's perfectly safe."

I suspected Ana Lane was many things.

Perfectly safe wasn't one of them.

I glanced past the kid to the windows of the ice cream shop, where a garish selection of Milk Way branded clothing hung on display. I ground my teeth together, debating what to do.

Ana Lane wasn't my problem.

I shouldn't get involved.

I was the shark for crying out loud, not the blasted lifeguard! And I still had a body to dump.

But I knew all too well what trolled the dark water of the Cape at night, and all I could visualize was Pix, desperate to breathe as one of my kind slowly drew her soul from her body.

"Damn it!" I growled, my conscience apparently sliding back into place after a century and a half of being AWOL. How convenient.

The kid – MJ – stopped and looked back at me. "What did ya say?"

I let out a defeated breath and said something I never thought would come out of my mouth. "I'll take the cow-print swim trunk in the window."

MJ blinked at me, no doubt convinced I'd lost my mind, which was probably accurate at this point.

"Really? You mean the ones with *Milk Way Rules* on the back, or *Udderly Delicious*?"

"Surprise me," I moaned. MJ smiled wickedly and nearly skipped back to the shop to grab my new swimwear. I could almost hear Benton laughing at me from his toasty spot in Hell.

As soon as I convinced Pixie Pants to get out of the damn water, I was out of here. No way I was staying on the Cape past tonight.

No way. Never.

3

THE BITE OF THE frigid Atlantic was just what I needed to escape reality. To forget what waited for me at home if I returned before sunrise.

As I drove to Marconi beach, I convinced myself that the car could once again become my camper for the evening. I'd done it before, many times.

Too many times.

My father's scallop boat, *Miss Charlotte*, would shove off in a few hours, just before daybreak, and my father would be on board. For five days, he and his crew would be hunting shellfish and I'd be safe, if only briefly.

In years past, he could control it – the drinking, the lost days, the brittle hold he kept on his temper. But once I hit teenhood, he let the booze-induced demons win and they whispered to him one thing over and over: it was my fault.

My mother, gone from our lives, had disappeared into the night when I was just two years old. My father said she was a drug-addict – that the lure of the needle was a greater

22

reward than we were. It wasn't until he started drinking, that he began pointing fingers. He said the stress of having a child had pushed her over the edge.

That she'd left because of me.

And maybe that was true. Maybe she couldn't handle having a kid. Maybe she couldn't handle being married. The truth was, it didn't matter why she left, only that she did, and for that, I paid the price.

My dad was a good guy until that one fishing trip when he was introduced to the numbing void of alcohol. I don't know whether it was because it dulled his pain or made reality less sharp, but he quickly descended into THAT man – the one who sat in front of the TV, smashed out of his mind, entirely ignorant of the fact that we were once again without food and that the rain was beginning to seep through the neglected roof.

He once took such pride in our small, two-bedroom home. Now it was a shell of what it used to be, not unlike our lives.

At one time, Dad and I were awesome together. He'd read me stories at night and take me to the drive-in, giving me all his popcorn. He taught me to ride a bike and hit a curve ball.

He taught me to be brave.

But once the liquor took over, Jack Daniels became a greater joy than anything else in his life, including me.

I still held out hope that he'd eventually be willing to fight his way through the addiction and be the man he once was, but until then I needed to steer clear of his wrath – and the back of his hand.

MJ knew it too.

He'd seen the results all to clearly in the past. He wanted to call the police, but I begged him not to because I knew they would put me in foster care and Dad in jail. I needed to just make it to my eighteenth birthday, a little more than a year away, and I could move out. I could be free and get my dad help from a distance.

And so MJ agreed to keep my secrets and help hide the marks.

When I'd called him tonight at The Milk Way, I knew he was gonna freak out. My dad wasn't supposed to be home. He was supposed to have left earlier in the day to head out on the boat, but he hadn't. The fact that he was still at home when I drove up to the house could've cost me a black eye, except his truck tipped me off to his presence.

I'd been at RC Garage, working on a side job for crazy Dalca Anescu and her riding lawnmower. She was one strange lady, owning an herb and essence store known as The Crimson Moon.

People said she was a witch. Dalca claimed she was a Gypsy. I just thought she was basically nuts, but she also paid me well.

Jack, who owned RC where I worked, was a good guy. He allowed me to do side work on my own time, and let me stash the beat up Trans Am I was slowly restoring in the shed out behind the shop. Jack also let me keep all the money from the side work, though he could've very easily charged me a fee to use the space. He seemed to know that I was always in need of cash, no matter how much I worked.

My father's cut of *Charlotte*'s profits were usually donated to the local liquor store as soon as he stepped off the dock, so every dime I made paid for food, heat, lights, etc. I could tell that Jack knew something was up with my home life, but he never mentioned it.

So when I drove home and saw that Dad was still there, I dialed the docks and found out that *Miss Charlotte* had been rescheduled to leave tomorrow, instead of today.

That's when I called MJ and learned of Fat Head who believed anyone with ovaries couldn't turn a wrench. Pissed over his ignorance and determined to prove my worth, I had quickly climbed through my bedroom window, grabbed a few things, and headed to The Milk Way to kick some ass.

I was correct. The guy – Kian – was a TOTAL player and a rich brat to boot, especially with an Auburn. That car had to be worth at least five hundred thousand and was nearly the same as the one in the car museum in Sandwich.

Kian was also irritatingly handsome and at least six feet tall. Hell, he was not even a normal level of pin-up poster good looking. With his golden skin, god-like build, and short-cut blond hair, he was like a living, breathing Photoshop file for crying out loud!

He was probably as one dimensional as a computer file too, especially since I couldn't get a read on what he *really wanted* from me. Granted, I was still a novice at reading people's true desires, but I could almost always get a vague outline of what someone really wanted. Of course, being able to read someone was both a blessing and a curse when it came to my father. A blessing, because I knew he still loved me. A curse, because he seemed unable to pull his love through all the layers of hate and rage.

MJ used to joke that my ability was due to some freaky government experiment and that I'd escaped from their lab . . . or I was just another worker at 1-800-Psychic. He joked, until one day, while we were watching a movie, his skin became reflective.

Talk about an epic freak-out.

I damn near choked on my peanut M&Ms.

After digging through his family tree's many myths, he realized he had the ability to phase his body, which was what had caused his glitter-ball moment while watching Point Break.

Eventually (after some seriously messed up attempts that resulted in nightmare-worthy creations), MJ nailed a black dog form. I nicknamed him *Marsh*, short for his first name Marshall James, and he soon became known as the big, friendly town stray.

Yeah, MJ's ability made my gift as an emotional psychic *pale* by comparison.

So we formed our own support group, which consisted of just the two of us. We called ourselves "WA" for Weirdos Anonymous. We met exactly one time, got bored, and disbanded.

I smiled as the face of my dear friend popped into my head as he declared our first meeting "open" for business, only to realize we had no real business to discuss. Then we went surfing.

I finally pulled into the overlook parking lot at Marconi beach and saw a dozen or so people riding out into the silver waves. They always had extra boards for people to borrow, a fact which I was grateful of since I had to sell mine last year to catch up on the mortgage.

I slid out of the shop's rickety Ford that Jack was letting me use until the Trans Am was running, and quickly stripped out of my clothes.

In the dark, so far from the other surfers, I really didn't worry about someone getting an eyeful of my lady parts as I got into my zip-back bathing suit. I'd found the expensive board suit at a local thrift shop for just a few dollars, and it did a decent job of keeping me warm thanks to its high neck and long-sleeves.

Of course, certain less enjoyable classmates had laughed at my suit, claiming it was relic of their own grandmas' attics. And I admit, it did have a moth-bally smell when I first got it, but now it just smelled like the sea and me. More importantly, it could hide the occasional bruise.

It was one more layer of armor against the world.

Ready to ride, I jammed my boots under the back of my seat, but as I did so I felt something paper-like on the grungy floorboard. I picked it up, only to realize it was a wad of twenties – eighteen to be exact.

Three hundred and sixty dollars.

"Shit," I muttered, stuffing the money into a tear in the back seat. I bet my next meal that that guy, *Kian,* was half-way to Boston by now. The money was a windfall by my standards, but I didn't earn it and I didn't like pity.

He had thought I was broke. Took one look at my clothes and my ride and jumped to his own white-collared conclusions, figuring he could feed his thin morals by donating to the needy.

Pride made me want to hurl the wad of cash into the bonfire that flickered down near the water, but reality kept me sane.

I DID need the money. I WAS broke.

I kicked the door shut and locked it, angry at Kian for looking down at my crappy life from his privileged perch.

Jamming my keys up under the car's rusted frame, where they'd be hidden from sight, I finally headed toward my own form of therapy.

The long sweep of pine stairs that led from the dune to the rolling water was cold under my feet, and the air held the smell of the ocean in the restless wind. My hair snaked and twisted around my throat as I leapt to the sticky sand, soaking in the dampness and freedom that accompanied the endless waves.

Here, at the mercy of the unforgiving Atlantic, I controlled my fate. On the cusp of a perfect wave, the choice was mine alone: take the drop into the water's fury, or fall back into the safety of the trough.

In the distance I could see five or six surfers catching the metallic waves and bobbing in and out of the moonlight. We Howlers rarely spoke to one another while surfing. Rather, our emotions and desires were spelled out clearly with a simple nod or how we cut our boards into the backs of sea-born dragons.

That's what I called the surfers when I was a child – dragon riders.

My father used to tell me stories about ghostly mermaids, sharks that lived among us, and how the waves hid the arching backs of sea dragons. It was his way of connecting me to his work as a fisherman, and I could easily recall the feel of his heavy boots as I stomped around the house.

At one time my father's love was effortless, and I held fast to that knowledge by remembering his stories and the way he laughed at my wide eyes as he told them to me.

Looking out over the breakers, that's what I still saw – dragons, invisible to the human eye, bowing their backs to give birth to the waves. I'd never fail to see them and prayed that someday my father would see them too.

4

❧ KIAN ❧

AS I WATCHED MY car-fixing Pixie paddle out into another set of swells, I knew my list of regrets was going to be a mile long by dawn. The swim trunks, which were riding up in the most irritating way possible, were going to top that list – right after I torched them.

In my haste to get to Marconi, I'd left Benton in the trunk, which was NOT good. I needed to get rid of his body soon, otherwise he'd be permanently folded like a Chinese take-out box, which would definitely tip-off the coroner's office that he didn't actually overdose.

What the hell was wrong with me? I shouldn't be here, stalking some afterschool special with a bad case of "screw you" attitude.

So what if she gets herself killed?

So what if she has a kick-ass personality?

I'd slammed the door on whatever scrap of humanity I had left years ago. Centuries ago. For crying out loud, there was a dead guy still in my car!

His car.

Whatever.

But with one streak of lousy luck, I had come face to face with someone who was a curiosity to me. An oddity that burned like a vibrant green flame, setting her apart from everyone else. She demanded my attention, like a puzzle that dares to be solved, and weirdly, I wanted to know more about her.

Maybe I just like a worthy adversary, almost like a cat that stalks a cobra. Maybe I like the thrill of the hunt and the knowledge that the target of my semi-obsession has one hell of a bite.

Humans normally didn't do "it" for me. I liked my females flawless, stacked, with legs like a bluegrass filly. And Mortis females were like walking slices of Playboy perfection. The fact that they were egotistical, self-centered sociopaths was something I tended to overlook, thanks to their curves and deliciously loose morals.

Quite frankly, I liked the killer ladies because they were very much like me – selfish, wealthy, and hot. Hey, I'm not afraid to admit any of that because facts are facts: I'm built like Captain America and probably have more money than Marvel.

Except right now the cow print was kicking the crap out of my ego. I swear, if one of these weed-infested surfers made a single comment about the *Udderly Delicious* now on my ass . . .

I needed to leave. Turn around, RIGHT NOW, and get off the Cape. Toss Benton off the Sagamore Bridge and floor it all the way to Boston.

But as I watched Pix carve her way down the side of a wave, I knew I couldn't leave. I needed to unlock her secrets – decode *why* she had lured me in, and more importantly, *how*. And the only way I could do that was to keep her safe, at least for tonight. I assured myself that if she turned out to be a total dud, I'd leave her to her own defenses.

Survival of the fittest, and all.

I headed down the dunes to the beach, hoping to steer clear of the handful of humans dotting the area. Pix had chosen a more remote stretch of water, placing herself a football field's distance from most of the other surfers.

In one way, I was thrilled she was farther from the others since I wouldn't be forced to give EVERYONE a nice display of my beachwear. On the other hand, being by herself made her a bigger target.

Riding solo in the waves, she was exactly who I would've tracked to kill. Someone who kept to themselves and whose death would remain off the radar for a little while. Someone whose existence was not acknowledged by those around her. The fact that none of the other surfers seemed to pay her any attention, made my chest feel tight. I hated the sensation.

Would anyone care if she died?

Would anyone mourn her?

5

"WOW. DID YOU SLEEP at all or just hang-ten all night?" asked MJ from behind the counter as I dragged my exhausted butt into the Milk Way at 6am. I let the faded screen door slam back into place behind me, scattering the drowsy moths by the outside light.

I slumped into one of the retro stools.

"Thanks for the pep-talk," I yawned, sliding my hand out over the faded countertop, turning my arm into a pillow. I could fall asleep, right now. Instantly.

Last night I'd been plagued by a freakish instinct that someone was watching me – ALL NIGHT LONG. While it was probably an owl or a hungry coywolf, it freaked me out enough to scare away any decent sleep.

Prying one eye open when I heard MJ sigh, I found myself staring at a sweaty offering of orange juice.

I studied the watery lines that slid down the side of the drink, trying to discern the imperfections in the glass that caused the drips to zigzag every once in a while.

"You should've stayed at my house. My mom wouldn't have cared," he scolded, watching me as he placed a few slices of chocolate chip bread into some electric oven thing. I pulled myself back up to sitting, stretching as I did so in a vain attempt to perk up.

I had to be at work in an hour. Ugh.

I wasn't willing to attempt a shower at home on the chance that *Charlotte* was still in slip 12 at the Barnstable docks. While Dad should be long gone by now, I was determined to wait until after work to finally head back to our house and scrub the salt and seaweed from my body. Then I'd collapse on my mattress and sleep for twelve hours straight in the silence of the house.

That's all it was to me anymore – just a place to crash when my Dad was away or sober, which was unpredictable at best.

Winter was going to be a challenge, as it always was. Sleeping in the car wouldn't be such a great idea when the temperature dropped, leaving my house the only real option and a dangerous game of Russian roulette.

Sneaking inside when I suspected Dad had been drinking was the only way I stayed safe in my room. Often, he was too bombed to know I was there, hiding among my threadbare stuffed animals with the bureau up against the door. Hell, I suspected he was too bombed to even care where I was.

But every once in a while, we ended up colliding when he was drunk. My body tensed at the memory of the last time he lost control and I was in his way. After that, MJ and I installed a heavier door to my room, complete with dead bolt.

I still used the bureau however – a silent defender against the rage that randomly lurked inside my house.

I looked out the wall of windows that framed the Milk Way. The fog that had set in from the night before drifted down the road like a parade of children seeking mischief. It slipped through the hedges and fences of the antique homes, and gathered in damp, sticky pockets around the street lamps, only to be shooed along by the morning breeze.

Inside the Milk Way, the walls were plastered with posters of upcoming events and photos from patrons and workers. There were newspaper clippings and clothing strung haphazardly over the ceiling, and the blackboard was riddled with flavors and specials.

Nothing here had changed in decades and it was the closest I'd ever come to having a home that welcomed me without question. I owed this sanctuary to MJ and his folks.

Unfortunately, the boobs and butt I had finally sprouted meant sleep-overs had officially become forbidden by MJ's mom. "We aren't in elementary school anymore, MJ. Your mother would freak out to have me bunking at your house, and you know it."

"You could've just snuck in."

"Oh yeah – because THAT wouldn't make her suspicious at all! If she ever found out I'd bunked on your floor, she would totally think we were . . . you know."

"Trying to make babies?" He gave me a wink as he pulled two thick loaves from the toaster. God bless the Nirvana coffee shop down the street that delivered daily to the Milk Way.

"Exactly," I replied as MJ placed the steaming bread in front of me, complete with a silver ice cream dish of vanilla butter. Just the smell of the oven-baked chocolate was enough to make me want to lick the counter. I slathered on a heaping portion of butter and started to devour my breakfast.

MJ leaned against the counter, watching me stuff my face. "You slept in the car again?" he asked, all humor falling away.

I didn't take my eyes off my meal and nodded. I could feel him watching me. Could feel the sadness in his gaze.

I didn't have time to feel sorry or sad – I just needed to plow forward and I'd be okay. And my dad would be okay too.

Someday I'd fix him, I was certain. I just needed to get through the next few months, start junior year at Barnstable and keep to the background. By next summer, I'd be eighteen and could help him get sober.

Thirteen months was all that stood between me and independence.

And once I was officially an adult, Dad would see, finally, how bad he was when he drank. He would realize that he needed to stop drinking and I could help him, all while living safely in the apartment above RC garage.

Well . . . there wasn't an apartment there *yet*, but I knew I could convince Jack that I could turn the old storage area into a tidy, studio living space.

Everything was going to be all right. I had to believe everything was going to be okay. I wiped my lips and stuffed the paper napkin into the empty glass as I got up.

"Thanks for the food, MJ. I've gotta get to work, but wanna catch up later? Maybe rent a movie?" MJ knew my dad's fishing schedule as well as I did. He demanded to know once he realized I wasn't just a clutz, often falling against the stairs or doorframe.

"Sounds good. I'm done by eight tonight. Want me to grab the movie?" he asked, glancing behind him at the sound of a door banging shut in the back room and his mother's voice calling to him. "I'm out front with Ana, Mom!" he yelled back.

MJ's mom appeared through the swinging backroom doors, her arms loaded with files. "Good morning, Ana. How's things?"

"Good, Mrs. Williams. How are you?" I replied.

"Oh you know – busy. Always busy," she replied, stretching on her tip-toes to try and give MJ a peck on the cheek. He leaned down to her under five-foot frame and was smooched by his mom, who then hurried upstairs to the office. Though MJ looked nothing like his Chinese mom, he did get his shifting ability from her side of the family. His mom, however, didn't know that her son barked at cats once in a while.

41

"I've gotta fly. I'll see you tonight," I said, heading to leave, but as I began pushing the screen door open, I noticed that there was a gap between some of the Milk Way branded clothing.

The horrible pair of cow-print swim trunks was missing.

MJ and I had made a bet over those awful things the day his mom hung them up. I bet him five dollars they'd never sell and his mother would make HIM wear them as advertising. MJ said that they would sell someday, because tourists were just that weird.

I pointed to the gap in the clothing and looked at MJ. "You're kidding, right? Did someone ACTUALLY buy them?"

"YUP," he chirped with a huge smile. "You owe me five bucks!"

I shook my head. "Who in the heck would've ever bought those?"

MJ had the most ridiculous, Joker grin plastered on his face. "Let's just say that Mr. Fancy Car has a thing for bovines."

I blinked. "Are you serious?"

MJ nodded.

"Dear heavens . . . he really is a pervert," I muttered as I dug five ones from my back pocket and slapped them down on the counter.

As I left, I heard MJ cheerfully yell to his mom something about winning a bet.

6

I was officially done pinching automobiles from drug dealers.

I'd spent the night watching over Pix's car, but just before dawn I decided I needed to finally get rid of Benton. Unfortunately, it wasn't until I was at a nearby beach, ready to drag his body to the surf, that I noticed the powder in the bottom of the trunk. It seemed to be spilling from a panel near the wheel-well and I soon realized that Benton wasn't the only thing stuffed in the vehicle.

The Auburn was a rolling buffet of cocaine.

I'd heard of the cartel using cheap model cars to bring drugs over the border, stuffing their wares in every door panel, tire, and seat, but using a half-million dollar vehicle was a new one for me.

Determined to distance myself from whatever major illegal activity Benton was wrapped up in, I took him and his car back to his house and parked it in the garage. I propped Benton up behind the steering wheel like a moldy mannequin and left on foot.

The cops and the feds were going to be all over his death once someone found him. And hell only knows how many other drug dealers he was connected to. For all I knew, his death could cause a domino effect among the drug kingpins. No thanks – I didn't need to get wrapped up in that nonsense.

I walked through the town, now car-less, watching paperboys deliver the news and early risers sip coffee from porches. There was a peacefulness to the morning – a quiet that blanketed Cape Cod with a sort of untouchable reverence. In the early morning, cars didn't clog the roads and children weren't yet up, shouting and playing.

It was the type of world that welcomed me – silent, shadowed, and misty.

Somehow I ended up standing in front of Elizabeth Walker's home, studying the grand porch and towering roof. It was obvious that no one lived here anymore, and I wasn't sure anyone had since her death.

Though it was just a house, it was also a symbol of a time when I was still human. When I was the golden son to a ship building family and I was set to marry a young woman named Mary. Though she adored me, I admit that I was less than loyal, even back in the 1840s. But Mary's family represented a powerful alliance for my family, and thus we were matched to marry – she was seventeen and I was twenty.

And then the night of Elizabeth's Christmas party happened and I ended up a Mortis by morning . . . and Mary was dead within a day because of me. Less than a year later, I watched Elizabeth die in the arms of a powerful Mortis named Jacob Rysse – he was a clan leader, and I was one of his soldiers.

I did my best to distance myself from those memories – harden my heart to the suffering and the death. For the most part, it was easy. But on rare occasion, I ran up against the past in the form of a Mortis named Raef Paris, and the memories came rushing back.

He had built Elizabeth's house, and as I studied the strong lines and perfect angles, I had to give him credit – he was a great carpenter, even at eighteen. But that party also marked the end of his human life as well – turned, like me, into a soul thief.

He too was drafted into Rysse's clan and stood beside me the night Elizabeth died.

Like most Mortis, he kept to himself, but every once in a while I would see him in some random bar in some random city. In those moments, I was back on the Cape with Mary and Elizabeth and my parents and every sin I committed against those who trusted me. Being in front of Elizabeth's house had the same effect on me.

Being with Pix also felt oddly similar, but with her, the pain didn't exist. Whereas Raef and the house dragged me back to the past, Pixie seemed like a chance at the future.

A chance to be different.

I looked down the street towards the Milk Way and wasn't all that surprised to see a familiar, beat up blue Ford parked by the front door. The sight of her car, sitting among the drifting fog, gave me something I hadn't felt since the days when I was human.

Hope.

7

ANA

THE DAY WAS GOING to be murderously hot. Sweat had already begun to mingle with the rust and grime that was slowly spreading over my coveralls, like a mold that could defy Mr. Clean.

I wiped my brow with the back of my hand, but my hair stuck like Super Glue to my cheeks. Even worse, it had taken on a hay-like consistency thanks to the salt water from last night's surfing.

What a thrill.

Jack tried to get me to come into the air-conditioned office and eat my lunch, except there was one problem: I didn't have a lunch to eat.

Plus, Corbin, the other mechanic whose greatest claim to fame was getting tossed out of college last year due to some stunt-gone-wrong, always checked out my rack. A few weeks ago, he even went so far as to congratulate me on my small boobs because, apparently, they were the "perfect handfuls." When he offered to prove his point, I nearly hurled a socket wrench at his head, but Jack got between us.

So lunch, for me, was best spent tucked under the chassis of the Trans Am I was slowly restoring. Jack had inherited it from a customer who traded it for some work on his motorcycle. Realizing I was drooling over it the moment it was towed out back, Jack agreed to let me have it, in return for working half-days on Saturday for free. I jumped at the chance to have something so beautiful that I could call my own.

Well . . . it *would be* beautiful when I was done with it. Right now it was one cylinder away from the junkyard.

I sung silently to the *Fall Out Boy* song playing through my elderly iPod's ear buds as I worked, urging the rusted bolts out of the oil pan one by one.

Lost in the music and my work, I didn't realize I was no longer alone in the garage until someone squeezed my leg. I jumped, startled, and banged my head against the car's frame, swearing.

Corbin was such an ass.

I yanked the ear buds out of my ears and began pulling myself out from under the car, yelling at Corbin as I did so.

"You're such a moron! Keep your skeevy hands away from me or I'll unscrew a whole new set of balls from your body! Do you hear me, Corbin?" I demanded, finally sliding out from under the car.

Standing over me, a look of pure amusement on his face, was the dude from last night. I was stunned into silence for a moment, but then narrowed my eyes as a confident, irritating smile spread on his lips.

He offered a hand to help me up. "We covered this before, but I'm Kian, not Corbin. And in my defense I did call your name at least five times. How's your head?"

"Dented, obviously, because I must be hallucinating. As far as I can recall, you were headed out of town," I replied, rubbing my forehead as I got to my feet, refusing to accept his help. I tossed the wrench on my tool cart with a *clang*, and he tucked his hands into his designer khakis, watching me. I noted that he hadn't changed since last night and I wondered what he did with the swim trunks. "What do you want?"

"What? No question of concern at all? No curiosity as to whether or not your automotive skills got me past the harbor without major engine failure?"

"My skills are flawless, thanks. I know what I did under your hood last night."

"Do you say that to all the guys you rescue from the side of the road?" he asked, smiling. I blushed, fiercely, which only pissed me off more.

"Ya know what? I don't need to be harassed anymore than I already am, so why don't you cough up the reason you're here or move your ass along."

Something odd crossed his face for a moment, as if he was thinking of asking me something, but then he seemed to pull back. He cleared his throat and slid into a more business-like mode.

"I'm looking for a car to buy and I thought I could pay you to help guide my selection. I entirely trust your fine skills under any hood I have."

Ha! I bet you do. "You should buy a Pinto. Hatchback. It suits you."

"Trust me – the storage on those things is *way* too small and the car, way too crappy. I don't think so."

"What the hell happened to the Auburn?"

He leaned against the edge of the open bay door, the hot sun making his golden hair take on a halo effect. "I had borrowed it from a . . . friend of a friend. I had to return it last night."

"Did you leave the *Udderly Delicious* swim trunks in it as well?"

He actually smiled, and the way his face lit up nearly made my heart twist. "Oh no. I kept those. They're one of a kind – at least, if there's a scrap of mercy in the world, they WILL BE the only ones ever made."

I laughed. I couldn't help it. Kian was everything that I avoided, and while he may not be as loaded as I once thought, he was still wearing beautifully made clothing and was shopping for a car.

He was still one of them. One of those guys.

As I looked him over, from his looming height to his sculpted body, I realized I was probably nothing more than a game to him. I was a "wrong side of the tracks summer

"Um. Are you okay?" she asked.

Hell, NO I wasn't all right! It had to be a lie — such bonds are supernatural fairy tales. I was in control of my destiny. I could walk away. I could pull out and leave her standing on the docks whenever I wanted.

Pix smiled a little. "'Cause you look like you might barf, and no offense, I don't want to be barfed on. The two hundred a day does not include puking rights." She smiled a little. "Plus we're only stuck on the boat for maybe another ten minutes. Just keep your eye on the distance — it eases the seasickness."

I wasn't seasick — I was heartsick — but I did as she instructed because looking at her was too hard. Because looking at her reminded me of all the reasons I was wrong for her and all the selfish reasons why I didn't care.

I was going to stay.

Find a way to be part of her world.

I looked back at her and she gave a lopsided smile. "See? You look a little better. Told ya — keeping your eye on the horizon helps. Barf-incident avoided. I totally earned a tip!"

Oh, hell.

I'd become bonded to the soul of Ana Lane.

10

HOLY CAR HEAVEN.

The little fishing port of Edgartown had exploded into candy apple red, electric blue, and midnight black. The cobblestone streets were lined with chrome and glass and steel, all formed into the most amazing examples of every muscle car that had raced through my daydreams since childhood. America definitely had an addiction to fine automobiles, and I was probably the lead junkie.

I could feel Kian's eyes on me as I wandered through the rows of cars, chattering on endlessly about the finer points of a given vehicle's history, the uniqueness of an engine, and the general FREAKIN' AWESOMENESS that was everywhere.

I was expecting him to tease me about my ridiculous fan-girling over horsepower and carburetors, but instead he was attentive. He really listened, asking questions and trusting my instincts as I rambled and gushed, but he never stopped me.

Her words were cut off by a young guy calling her name and waving wildly from across the street. "ANA! Hey, ANA!"

Pix finally spotted the caller a few seconds after I had, and a huge smile spread on her face. She waved and the kid ran across the street, grabbing her in a hug. I tensed and something that felt strangely like jealousy slipped through my veins.

"Girl! What the hell are you doing here? Are you scoping out new toys for Waite?"

Ana shook her head, still radiant with happiness. "No, no! I'm here as an, uh . . ." she looked at me, trying to figure out what exactly I was to her. I needed to define that once and for all . . . as soon as I figured it out.

"She's here as a friend, whose top notch skills as a mechanic I'm using to my full advantage. Hi – I'm Kian O'Reilly," I said, offering a hand to shake. The kid didn't hesitate and gave a firm shake in return.

"Nice to meet ya – I'm Seth. Ana and I work for Lawson Waite. He's got loads of cash and spends it on loads of cars, which is where we come in. He's like the island's very own Jay Leno, except, well – he looks like a skinny nerd."

Ana laughed and looked up at me, offering an explanation. "Seth works full time for Mr. Waite, but I help out as needed. He's an investor and my Dad took out a loan from him for his business. That's how I met him."

"I see," I replied, easing myself a little closer to Pix, as if I could define her as a piece of property I'd optioned. "Mr.

Waite sounds like someone I could probably get along with. Is he like a rock star? Big parties and buckets of champagne?"

Seth laughed, "Yeah, that would be a big, fat 'no.' With the exception of the guard dudes that are always at his place, the guy is pretty boring."

Ana nodded.

Suddenly, I didn't like Mr. Waite so much. Men with bodyguards and lots of money usually have enemies – enemies that aren't exactly law abiding citizens. "What's with the bodyguards?" I asked.

Seth shrugged. "Word is that he was mugged once. I mean, he travels a lot and he's worth a fortune. Given that Ana could probably flatten him into a pulp, I get why he wants some hired muscle with him."

Pix played with her ponytail, pulling a piece of fluff from a purple strand. "Waite is nice to me when I go there – well, when I see him anyway. I don't go up to the main house very often. I hang out in his sick garage."

"With ME!" Seth grinned.

I was not thrilled with the arrangement at all.

"Speaking of hanging out, any chance you could swing up to Waite's with me and check out what is going on with his '59 Electra? It cranks over, runs for five minutes or so, then dies. I've been through everything." Seth looked hopeful.

Ana stuck out her tongue, acting disgusted. "God – he still has that thing? That is the ugliest car on the planet. Can't we just declare it dead and bury it?"

"Sorry, but Waite wants it running. Can you come and add your sexy, brilliant head to our motley crew?"

Yeah – I really didn't like Seth.

Ana looked up at me, then back to her friend, wincing. "I'm sorry Seth, but I can't. Kian just grabbed the '63 Sting Ray and we're going to go celebrate and then we have to grab the ferry back. I just don't have time."

Seth raised an eyebrow. "Ferry? What ferry? All the boats have been cancelled until tomorrow. Roughs seas from an offshore storm. You ain't going anywhere with that Corvette until tomorrow."

Ana's eyes went wide. "When did they cancel?"

"A couple hours ago. Lemme guess – you don't have a room booked, do ya?" Seth was irritatingly delighted.

"DAMN!" she moaned, turning to me. I loved the fire in her blue eyes, even if it was fueled by frustration. "There won't be a single room left by now. I'm sorry, Kian, but I hope you like sleeping on the beach."

"Or in a 1963 Sting Ray," added Seth, totally chipper. "On the plus side, now you DO have time to come and bail out my butt with Mr. Waite."

I watched Ana and she looked torn on what to do.

There was a loyalty to her that I respected and it was pulling her in two different directions. I wasn't thrilled with this Waite guy, and Seth was definitely checking out Ana for more than her mechanical skill, but I also couldn't just tell her I already had a room. She'd figure out that I'd planned to stay on the island all along, and that tentative friendship we were starting to build, would implode.

I didn't want to let her go, but I had no choice.

I touched her fingertips, and she looked up at me, surprised. "Listen, Pix – it's okay if you want to go and check on the car with Seth. I'll look for a place where we can stay for the night. I can pick you up in the Vette – how long do you think you'll need?"

"I . . . uh . . . Are you sure? I mean, I feel like I'm stealing from your piggy bank. You're paying for me to work for you, not someone else."

Seth gave me a weird look, probably trying to figure out what exactly I was buying from Ana Lane. The thoughts, which I knew were running through his head, made me want to squeeze his skull like a stress ball.

"No – it's fine. Just give me a time and place, and I swear I'll be there," I assured her.

She smiled at me as she rattled off an address in Lower Makonikey. "I'll be waiting for you out by the main gate at 8pm. Don't be late, Mr. O'Reilly," she instructed, her smile growing.

"I'm never late, Ms. Lane. Never."

"Overachiever," she accused, poking me in the side, but I grabbed her hand, stopping her. In that instant, something flickered over her face – something that looked like longing and hope mixed together. "What can I say? You bring out the best in me."

"I try," she whispered, a little dazed.

74

"I'm here for a pick up," I said, hoping my vague response might give me insight into what Waite was really up to.

The guy narrowed his gaze, "We've got no scheduled pick ups tonight." I heard the click of a gun being cocked and glanced in the sideview mirror to see Thug 2 easing his firearm from his holster.

I didn't need this to go south right now – not when I had no clue where Ana was inside the sprawling estate. "I'm here to pick up Ana Lane – she's a mechanic here."

The change in demeanor of the two gun-toting gate keepers was instant. Thug 1 relaxed as Thug 2 slipped his gun back into its holster. "You're here for Rosie, huh? You must be some kind of brave to take her on."

"Rosie? No, I'm here for Ana. ANA LANE," I stressed, starting to worry I just blew her cover or something.

Thug 2 laughed, placing the mirror back in the gatehouse. "No, no. We call her Rosie like *Rosie the Riveter*. The girl is fierce. Stupid here tried to ask her out once. Once!" he laughed, thumbing toward Thug 1, who nodded.

"That girl has a razor sharp tongue. She scared the crap out of me."

I smiled, thinking of Ana hurling her ego crushing opinions at either of these two morons. I pointed at the gate, "So, can I go get her?"

Thug 2 shook his head. "Sorry man, gotta wait here. We'll call down to the garage and get her to walk up."

I nodded, "Should I stay here, or . . ."

"Here's fine," said Thug 1, no doubt determined to keep an eye on me. I wanted to ask them about the extreme security measures, but I feared my curiosity would set them off and I'd never get Pix out.

I needed to remember that she'd been coming and going from here without incident for a while. I needed to not rock the boat, or she could pay the price.

So I kept up small talk with the two guards, my eyes scanning the rolling lawn as I waited for Pix, who eventually appeared over the rise with Seth in tow.

She reached the gatehouse and Thug 1 and 2 wished her goodnight. Seth gave her a wave from behind the gate as I held open the door to the Vette for her.

"Thanks again, Ana!"

"No worries, Seth!" called Pix as she slid into my car.

I waved to the guards as I got in the drivers side and backed away from Waite's estate and whatever underhanded business he was really dealing in.

"Thanks for picking me up," she said to me, a smile on her face.

"Anytime. Car all fixed?" I asked, thrilled she was safely tucked into my car and no longer hidden on Waite's property.

"Of course. Do I ever fail?" she snorted, crossing her arms in defiance.

"Somehow I doubt failure is an option with you, Pix. Oh, and dinner is behind your seat."

the Flying Horses' barn, tipsy from the carousel and one another.

Suddenly, Kian stepped out from an alleyway in front of me. Shocked, I tripped forward, nearly crashing into him, but he grabbed me with lightning fast reflexes.

How in the hell did he get ahead of me?

"Pix – what are you doing?" he asked, confused as he let me go. "Did I say something to offend you?"

I shook my head and started past him, but he grabbed my hand, halting me. "Slow down. I can't help you if you won't tell me what is going on in that head of yours."

"I'm not your charity case, Kian," I snapped, emotions messing with my temper.

I pulled my hand free and concern creased his forehead. "What makes you think I see you as a charity case?"

"Oh please! The extra money in my car? The trip over here? The room? Let's face it – you and I are from two different tax brackets. Hell, we're from two different galaxies. We don't work, you and I."

Kian carefully took a step forward, as if he was worried I'd run again. "You don't know that, and help from a friend is not charity."

I tossed my hands in the air, frustrated. "Oh my god! You're impossible! Look, you can't help me, all right? I have a goal – a finish line. If I can just make it there, everything will be okay. And you – you complicate things." I sighed, studying our surroundings, but refusing to look at him.

People still flowed by us, once in a while paying us a curious look as we stood like statues on the sidewalk.

Finally Kian spoke. "What's the goal, Pix? Where's the finish line?"

I shook my head, not wanting to answer him as I fiddled with my rope bracelet.

He reached out and touched my chin, turning my face to look at him. "I won't tell your secrets, but I need to know where you're running to. As your friend, I deserve that much."

Memories of my dad began playing through my mind: the good, the bad, and the brutal. I'd survived this long without telling anyone, except MJ, what my life was really like, and Kian couldn't become part of that inner circle. He could end up reporting my dad, and everything that I'd worked so hard to avoid would land right on my doorstep.

I swallowed. "The future. A better future."

He seemed to turn that answer over in his head. "What if you only get today?" he asked.

I crossed my arms. "Then I got this far, in one piece and on my own."

"Do you like to always be on your own? I mean, I know you're friends with the ice cream cowboy, but don't you want . . . oh, I don't know . . . a really hot guy with a sick car as a partner in crime?"

I couldn't help but smile, some of my tension slipping, and I finally met Kian's eyes with my own. "Partner in crime, huh? MJ could be a master criminal for all you know. You may be trusting his wholesome demeanor a little too much."

"Yeah, I don't think so. That kid is total vanilla, despite the fact that he was devious enough to sell me overpriced cow hide."

I laughed, Kian smiled, and just like that, he made the shadows in my life flee. He was so different from anyone I'd ever known, like a burst of oxygen in a room starved of air.

"Pix – even if all you'll let me be is your getaway driver, I'll be happy. And I can even overlook the stranglehold you have on your life and the fact that you've probably got a Daily Planner filled out for the next two decades. Just slate me in somewhere, will ya?"

I thought about the two of us, laughing and tormenting one another over the past two days and how much more alive I felt when I was with him.

A mutinous part of my mind whispered that maybe he didn't need to be a roadblock. Maybe he could just be a more scenic route to get to where I needed to be.

Mentally, I was fried. Making it to my eighteenth birthday, would be a test of sheer bone-grinding determination. Despite MJ's best efforts, I was getting exhausted, and lately I felt more alone than ever before.

Maybe Kian was placed in my path to save me from myself. Maybe I just needed to give up a little of my control.

I crossed my arms as I looked up at him. "I guess it's a free country. If you want to stay, who am I to stop you? But I'm busy – I work, I have a life." Well . . . a semi-life at least.

"You have a life?" he asked with a smirk.

I poked him in the chest. "Watch it, Frat Boy, or I'll evict thee from my corner of the Cape. And if you start following me around like a lost puppy, I'll kick your ass."

He snatched my finger, but then gathered the rest of my hand in his. "Jeez – your country sure sounds like a dictatorship."

I smiled evilly. "Where you're concerned, it's a monarchy and I'm the queen."

16

MJ'S EYES WERE SO huge, that I literally thought they might pop out of his head and roll around on the dirty garage floor.

"So, hold up – you're telling me that he managed to get you guys a room last night on the Vineyard, but HE slept in the car? Are you serious? The dude was a TOTAL player the other night!"

I shrugged, switching out sizes on my wrench. "I'm telling you, he isn't like the normal, rich turd that washes ashore every summer."

"Why? 'Cause he's a different shade of the same crap? Ana – please listen to me. Something is up with this guy – I just know it. I mean, seriously, who in their right mind lends a friend a half-million dollar car? NOBODY. And then he gets all tweaked about buying the swim trunks – and not just any ones, but the HIDEOUS ones – and wants to know about night surfing. He's not right! He could have, like, a split personality or something."

I climbed my way back up into sand-encrusted cab of classmate Teddy Bencourt's gigantic brown Ford pick-up, as MJ continued to list all the potential mental problems that Kian might be hiding.

I wedged myself back under the dashboard, securing the new, mega-watt stereo in place. Teddy had gotten it a few months back during some music festival and had been begging me to install it ever since. I was gleeful about the fact that Teddy, a huge kid and a linebacker for our football team, needed a girl to work on his testosterone-ridden ride. I rarely let him forget that I was his mechanic, going so far as to leave a little pink monster truck on his dashboard a year ago.

I smiled, noting that the toy still sat where I'd put it, thanks to the duct tape that Teddy had added to keep it in place.

"ANA! He could be a serial killer for crying out loud!" MJ's sudden appearance by my feet made me jump, and I dropped the wrench, just missing my eye.

"MJ! KNOCK IT OFF!" I snapped, sliding myself out from my place on the floormats. "He's not a freakin' serial killer. He's just some wealthy guy that needed some car help and now he wants to enjoy the Cape."

"Uh huh – and go for some lovin' in the dunes if you ask me. Have you forgot all about your goals? About getting the hell out of your house when you turn eighteen?"

MJ's blatant reminder of my hideous life smacked me hard in the chest, pissing me off. "Don't you DARE tell me that I've forgotten about my life! You go home, every night, and sleep fine knowing that your mom and dad won't flip the switch and knock you into the wall for eating the last bagel. You don't schedule your days around when the fishing is best and when the liquor store opens and closes. So don't you ever, EVER accuse me of forgetting about MY LIFE."

I was breathing hard, the skittering rage inside me causing my hand to tremble as I pointed accusingly at MJ. We rarely fought and the moment felt so foreign to me — so blinding and bitter at the same time.

I suddenly realized that Kian, without even trying, had put me at odds with my best friend. That couldn't happen. I wouldn't let it happen.

MJ looked at me sadly, his voice quiet. "You hurt enough Ana. More than anyone ever should, and I just don't want to see your heart get broken by this guy."

I dropped my hand and began to squeeze back under the dashboard, determined to finish Teddy's ride before dinnertime. I still had to deliver Dalca's lawnmower to the Crimson Moon, and had no desire to psychoanalyze my mental state with MJ at the moment. "I'm not giving Kian O'Reilly my heart, MJ. It's not even possible."

"Why is that?" he asked, leaning down so he could see me under the dash as I torqued in another screw.

"Because . . ." I sighed, "I've got nothing left to give."

* * * *

An hour later I was sitting next to Teddy in his truck, wondering if I was going to suffer permanent hearing damage.

"Girl, you dumb! This sounds lame!" he howled at the top of his lungs, trying to overcome 90 decibels of Flo Rida.

"WHAT? You don't like it?" I shouted, shocked he wasn't pleased. Heck, the system was so vicious you could shake the pinstripes off a car two towns over.

Teddy laughed at me. "I SAID, *YOU ARE DA BOMB! THIS SOUNDS INSANE!*"

I finally reached forward to the glowing stereo, turning down the sound, though the notes continued to ricochet around inside my skull. Dear god, I think my eyeballs were still vibrating. "I'm psyched you like it – it's a really nice system," I managed to reply. At least, I think I said it out loud, since I couldn't even hear my own voice.

"Boston Acoustics makes the sickest stuff," nodded Teddy. Even in his monster truck, his wide frame seemed to fill the space. He leaned forward, pulling a wad of cash from his back pocket and handing it to me. It was enough to get some groceries and pay a couple small bills.

I tucked the money into my pocket. "Thanks."

"Anytime, Lanes. So you think you can rig some speaker connections out the back of the cab? You know, for beach parties? I got some sick subwoofers at home that I want to stack in the back when we bonfire in the fall. Juniors, baby! Before ya know it, we'll be ruling the school as seniors!"

I snorted. "Ruling the school is a whole year away. I just want to survive junior year, thanks."

He gave me a light punch in the arm as he laughed. "As IF you even worry about surviving. You scare the tar out of every dude in school – well, except Williams, but he's an odd duck anyway. Seriously, though – you should work for a sports company testing their personal padding. If it can stand up to your foot, then it can take anything!"

Good grief, that story would follow me until the day I died. "First off all, that freshman was asking for it – no one accidentally grabs you in the butt like that and then asks you out. Secondly, I did not kick him in the balls. I kneed him. Big difference."

Teddy was roaring, slapping the faded dashboard with his huge hand. "He walked crooked for weeks, dumb kid!" he howled, nearly falling over with laughter.

He finally calmed down, a giant grin on his tanned face. "So, hey – listen – I'm having a house party tonight. Seven-ish. Music, food, and a bonfire on the beach. My place has a great view of the fireworks. Can you come? Drag Williams along too, and tell him to bring some Maple Walnut ice cream. My mom loves that stuff."

A party. I was an anti-party type of girl. Actually, I was fairly anti-social in general. I liked to be alone, away from the crowds and craziness. But I loved the Barnstable fireworks and Teddy's home was right on the beach – a perk of being part of a family that owned one of the most famous glass blowing companies in the country.

"I don't know . . . I'm not really – "

"Wait! Don't say no! Look, I'll even bribe ya!" I gave him a weird look as I watched Teddy yank his backpack off the floor and dig around in its front pocket. Finally he pulled out a small brown box and put it on the dash in front of me.

He sat back, arms crossed, looking mighty proud.

"What's this?" I asked.

"My dad let me work some scrap glass the other night. Check it out – I made it for Cara, hoping she'd finally say yes to a date, but I'm starting to think she plays for the other team . . . if ya know what I mean."

"Cara plays for both teams, Teddy. Trust me," I replied as I picked up the box, opening it carefully. Within was a solid ball of clear glass, about the size of a baseball. Fused inside was what looked like a cresting wave – as if Teddy had managed to trap Atlantis in an orb of ice.

"Teddy it's . . . incredible. It's a paperweight, right?"

He nodded. "Yup – I call it THE WAVE."

"How original," I chuckled. "Are you sure you want me to keep it?"

"Absolutely, though it *is* totally a bribe to get you to come to the party tonight. Plus, I know you use those stupid rocks to hold down the repair slips on your workbench. Not cool."

I rolled the ball in my hand, feeling its smooth surface turn against my palm as I tried to quiet my practical thoughts.

I was a teenager.

Parties should be the norm and I should try new things.

I mean, I went dancing – DANCING – with Kian. When the heck would I have ever done that in the past? And did the world implode because I hit the dance floor with a hot vacationer?

Nope – the world was still spinning, though Hell was totally vacationing on a glacier, because I was about to do the unthinkable.

"FINE! I'll come to your party, BUT I've first got to get over to the Crimson Moon and drop off a tractor. I might be late."

Teddy fist-pumped the air, but then paused. "You're going to Anescu's place? That lady is a whack-job, I swear! That place of hers is actually a candy cottage and she's just sitting there, like a black widow, trying to lure in the kids so she can shove them in the oven and make teenager-pie. *Here, Sonny want a piece of CANDY?*" he squeaked in the worst rendition of Dalca I'd ever heard.

"She's not some creepy old witch. She's just eccentric and she's nothing but nice to me. People need to give her a break."

"Ana, you have a dangerous soft-spot for lost causes."

"Obviously, because I agreed to come to YOUR party."

He laughed, "YEAH! Which is totally awesome! My fly skills with the glass furnace worked, huh?"

"Yup," I replied, placing the breakable bribe back in its box.

Teddy smiled as he watched me. "So, would ya also go on a date with me?"

"Nope."

He looked confused. "But I didn't grab you in the butt."

"It's still a 'no' Teddy."

17

THE CRIMSON MOON did have a Hanzel and Gretel forbidden-cottage vibe going on, but I blamed it on the abundance of plant life. Dalca was a level-ten tree hugger who let nature take over her house and the attached store, covering most of the shingles in a network of emerald vines and lavender flowers.

It was actually quite beautiful and Hobbitesque, except for that one time I face-planted into a huge spider web near the back door . . . and couldn't find the spider. I nearly stripped naked in my panic, sure a tarantula was hitching a ride on me somewhere.

Honestly, smaller spiders were okay in my book, but I knew Dalca prided herself on her organic lifestyle, including the use of huge web spinners to keep away the bad bugs. And Dalca's spiders would eat Alvin and the Chipmunks as a snack.

Bleh.

I backed the delivery truck down behind the shop's narrow stone driveway and unloaded the tractor, pushing it over to the small shack near the edge of her property.

I took a minute to catch my breath and looked out over the expanse of land that belonged to Dalca. The sweep of wildflowers that clutched the hillside spilled downward toward the ocean, scattering under the drifting bows of an awesome weeping beech tree. Every once in a while, I wandered out to that tree and walked the inner perimeter, searching for butterflies in the soft leaves.

That tree was its own secret garden and I loved it.

"Ana? Is that you?" called Dalca from her backdoor, half hidden by the vines. "Get in here and have some coffee!"

"Yup! I'll be right there!" I replied, jogging towards the house. As I reached the back door, I eyed the spider-hiding branches carefully and hurried inside.

"So how's business been?" I asked as I walked through the shop, seeking my semi-employer. Her voice carried easily from the backroom that was her kitchen.

"Pretty good, dear, pretty good! Come see what I got at the estate sale in Provincetown last weekend!"

I followed Dalca's voice towards her kitchen, admiring the fairy-like shop with its twinkling crystals and branches that hung from the ceiling, and the wealth of multicolored glass vials and books that jammed every inch of her shelves. As I entered the kitchen, I could smell the oven fresh bread she'd been baking, and the coffee as it brewed.

An animal soul was an acceptable substitute for a human, but nowhere near as potent. A human life was the ultimate high, sometimes lasting a soul thief a few weeks at a time. I, however, wanted no chance of developing cravings for souls around Pix, so the regular animal hunts would have to do for now.

I could also get some corpse blood from the coroner in Boston if I got really desperate, shooting it up with a needle like heroine. Blood carried a small amount of life force at all times, even after death, so it could be used in an emergency. The effects, however, didn't last long at all – it was a cracker, when you really needed a four-course meal.

I'd heard of some soul thieves who were so badly injured that they were forced to drink it, but there was no way I'd ever get that desperate.

Hell. No.

I watched as a few of the dock workers scrubbed down the side of a Donzi speedboat, talking to one another as they worked. While I didn't envy their crappy human lives, I did miss being on the water.

My family's wealth was forged on the back of the Atlantic, which was how I first met Elizabeth Walker. Her husband, Josiah, was a sea captain who had commissioned my family to build his newest ship. I'd brought drawings of the ship's layout to his home, and Elizabeth had answered the door.

Back then, she was the most magnificent young woman I'd ever seen – even more beautiful than Mary. I remember how she smiled and let me in, offering me tea and cookies as we waited for Captain Walker to get home. After that day, I became a regular at their parties at the insistence of Elizabeth. She was smart, funny and fearless, even around the most influential of men.

I rubbed my face, attempting to erase the visions of her alive – and dead – from my mind.

Damn, I needed some air.

I stepped from the Corvette and headed to the docks to admire the yachts. The long line of million dollar boats were all sporting a vast array of new designs and features that made them brilliant rebels on the ocean.

Farther down the dock, I noticed five well-dressed men standing on the back end of a stunning yacht with a ruby hull. They were holding papers and a man on the aft deck seemed to be taking note of who was there.

I approached one of the men in a Ralph Lauren suit. "What's going on?" I asked.

He looked me over for a moment, pushing his sunglasses back up his narrow nose, no doubt wondering why a guy as young as me was asking him questions. "The yacht is being auctioned," he replied shortly.

"Now?" I asked, realizing I may have just solved my current dilemma of room hunting.

"Yes. Now," replied the man, totally disgusted that I was still talking. I was going to shut down his arrogance in a big way.

I flagged down the auctioneer on the yacht. "I'll bid as well."

He glanced over to me. "Son — we have a reserve of two million on this vessel. Anything starting under that will be rejected."

I smiled, glancing once at Narrow Nose, and then back to the auctioneer. "That won't be an issue, sir."

The auctioneer looked a little surprised. "Come up here, son, and we'll see if we can qualify you to bid."

I climbed aboard the yacht and very quickly proved my worth thanks to my Black Card, a bank card so rare that not even billionaires could always get one.

After that, I was given a tour of the vessel, which was stunning and perfect for me — dark rich colors in shades of burgundy and black complimented the cherry wood and teak decking. A full gourmet kitchen, second wheelhouse, two bedrooms, and a designer bathroom made it a luxury hotel suite on the water.

Bidding lasted exactly two minutes, probably because I outbid everyone's top price by an easy million dollars, landing myself the ultimate bachelor pad on the water. I thought Narrow Nose was actually going to throw a temper tantrum and end up rolling around on the dock like a three year old.

As the bidders finally dispersed, mumbling unhappy observations my way, I signed the necessary paperwork with the banker, and was soon left alone.

I sat down on the white, aft lounge, smiling at my new digs. Of course, it did need a name.

I pulled my phone from my pocket, scrolling to the entry *Pixie Pants* and tapped the number she'd given me. It rang a few times and then I heard the phone pick-up.

I spoke before she could protest my calling. "So – you need to get your sassy butt to the harbor. And before you complain, I'm NOT nagging or stalking you. An opportunity presented itself, and I jumped on it, but I need your brilliance to come up with a name."

There was a moment of silence and then a guy responded. "Dude – this is Craigville Pizza. And I swear, if you're stalking me for some kinky reason, the police will never find your body. Now – do ya want a pizza or what?"

I quickly hung up the phone and sat there, stunned.

Ana Lane was the devil.

It would probably *not* be wise to ask for her help in naming my yacht, especially since she apparently gave me the number for the pizza shop, rather than her own.

Pix would name it all right.

Something like "Sucker" comes to mind.

19

ANA

I WATCHED MJ LOAD another quart container with Teddy's specified maple walnut ice cream, wondering yet again why my lean pal didn't sport giant biceps from his line of work. He was muttering about being dragged to a party that would be wall-to-wall jocks, and how they'd jammed him in the broom closet in middle school.

Truth was, I was still stunned I'd agreed to go.

Damn paperweight.

Damn Kian O'Reilly and his stupid *be selfish* chant.

"Ya do realize that Ted probably only invited me for the ice cream, right? I'm totally being used here," whined MJ.

"I'm NOT going alone. Plus, all you've got are a few moldy firecrackers and a cheap box of sparklers. I wanna see the big bangers, and Teddy's house has a great view."

MJ carried the two quarts to the counter and pressed on the logo tops while I shut the freezer bin behind him. "We don't even need to speak to anyone," I encouraged. "We can be hermits on the beach and just hang out by ourselves and eat all their food."

MJ shook his head. "We could just go to Bodfish beach and see the fireworks from there. We don't need to park our butts on Teddy's stretch of beach."

"If we went to Bodfish, there'd be half the world jammed onto the beach. At least at Bencourt's place, the beach is private."

I absolutely loathed how packed the beaches became in the summer, and during the Fourth of July it felt as though the air couldn't accommodate enough oxygen to sate the masses.

"Whatever," grumbled my pal. "So how was Dalca the Deviant this afternoon? Cooking up a witch's brew in the backroom?"

"She's not a witch, and no – no brew, though she got an antique coffee maker. Don't drink the motor oil she makes in *that* thing. She's still working out the kinks . . . I hope. She asked if we'd both been practicing our abilities. I told her summer was just too damn busy to work on, well, you know."

"Too busy to practice messing with people's emotions and chasing cats in dog form? Yeah, I know. I can barely come up for air from this place – we've been so busy this season," replied MJ, gesturing to the Milk Way in general.

"That's great though! Your folks must be pleased."

"They are, but I feel like I'm locked to this place. Sometimes I wish they'd just take that loan from Mr. Waite like your Dad did – you know, so they can hire a few more workers and let me breath."

MJ slid the ice cream into a paper bag and we headed out the door toward his Jeep. I was grateful his mom agreed to give him a few hours off – he really did live at the shop, and tonight it was packed.

I grimaced as I slid into the passenger seat of the Wrangler. "I don't know, MJ – sometimes I wish my Dad never got the loan from him. I feel like I'm obligated to fix his cars until it's paid off, and yeah – he pays me, but still."

"Do you ever even see Mr. Waite?" asked MJ, cranking the Jeep to life and pulling out onto Main Street. We drove past all the beautiful old homes with their tall, peaked roofs and widow's walks, heading for Old King's Highway. I envied the people that lived in the historic houses, wrapped in the past and privy to the history that whispered from the walls.

"Rarely. He's always traveling, though when I was at Dalca's today, she was talking about an estate sale she had attended for him. She said she was looking for some collectible thing for his museum."

"Collectible thing? Like what – a rare Pez dispenser?"

I laughed, "Uh, no. He collects cars, war relics, and like, old machinery things. Weird stuff too – like clocks and books. He's basically a really wealthy hoarder with good taste."

MJ snorted as he drove. "You know, if he's ever at a loss for where to burn a buck, you can tell him that he can toss it over here. I'll happily relieve him of a few grand anytime."

"Meeee too," I sighed, briefly imagining what it would be like to actually have enough money to pay all the bills for once.

20

 ANA

W ITHIN FIFTEEN MINUTES, MJ had turned onto Teddy's street and found a questionable parking spot half on the sidewalk, half on the road. Teddy's house looked like the movie theater when they re-released Jaws.

"Jeez – how many people did he invite?" I whispered.

MJ turned to me, his eyes wide. "I say we fling the ice cream through the front door and flee. Wadda ya say? We can still make it to Bodfish beach before the test shot."

I stared at the front of the gorgeous beach house. Its three stories of shingled, modern squareness were covered in acres of glass, which was totally appropriate for a family whose wealth was built on it. Lit from the inside and framed by the pink setting sun, it reminded me of the picture window at Kandy Corner, with the jars of rock candy and pulled taffy twinkling in the warm rays.

It was a crystal box, plucked from the Hollywood Hills and dropped into seaside Barnstable . . . and jammed with about fifty classmates inside, dancing and talking.

Maybe MJ was right. Maybe ditching now and running for Bodfish was the brightest idea.

I turned back to MJ, about to take him up on his idea when I spotted a very familiar '63 Sting Ray parked right on the lawn next to a large oak tree.

"Are. You. Kidding. ME?" I whispered, part pissed he was following me, part light-headed that I was going to see him again.

MJ looked at me, curious. "Chill, all right? If you want to go in, we can. Don't get your panties in a twist."

I shot him a death glare. "DON'T mention my panties. Ever. And secondly, Kian is here."

"WHAT?" MJ spun around, looking into the darkness of the yard where I was pointing. "How in the hell did he – AH!"

Screaming like a girl, MJ launched himself onto my lap when Kian banged on his window. I shoved him off me and glared out the window at Frat Boy, whose stunning face was smiling brilliantly. He gave a wave through the glass, then opened the door.

"Damn it – I nearly had a heart attack!" accused MJ, sliding back into his seat. Kian stepped back, leaning lazily on the open door frame.

"So, you girls stalking me or what?" he asked with a devilish smile.

I snorted, shoving my door open as MJ got out his side, forcing Kian to step back. He came around the Jeep to where I was standing, my arms firmly crossed. "What are you doing here?" I demanded.

"I'm staying for the summer, remember?" he replied, sly dog.

I poked him in the chest, nearly snapping my finger on his iron muscles. "I meant why are you HERE. At this precise location on the face of the planet?" MJ gave a fast nod, no doubt wondering as well.

"Word of mouth. And a party isn't a party without me. Plus, the pizza guy had plans."

I bit my lip trying not to smile. Plugging in the local pizza place's number was a spark of genius on my part. Plus, MJ ate so much of their buffalo pies, that the phone number was engraved in my brain. "Well that's a bummer."

"Isn't it? It's his loss though, and your gain."

MJ rolled his eyes just as I heard Teddy's voice echo across the manicured lawn. "Lanes! You made it!" he called, walking up to where the three of us stood. He looked at MJ, "Hey, Williams. Any chance you brought some ice cream?"

"As requested – I brought two full quarts."

Teddy gave him a punch in the arm and MJ did his best not to wince. "Thanks man! My mom will be stoked." Teddy then yelled back to his mom, who was setting out chips and salsa on the front porch. "MA! We have Maple Walnut from the Milk Way!"

Mrs. Bencourt waved to all of us. "Thank you, MJ!"

MJ waved back. "Sure – anytime. I'll just, uh, go find your fridge and jam it in the freezer." He then ditched us, leaving me to fend for myself with Kian and Teddy.

Traitor! I was going to revoke his sidekick status pronto.

"So Lanes – who's your buddy here?" asked Teddy, holding out a hand to Kian.

They shook as Stalker Boy introduced himself. "I'm Kian O'Reilly. I got word of the party from a couple of kids down by the harbor. Is it okay with your mom if I join the fun?"

"Hell yeah – the more the better. Hey, MA! It's cool that Kian here joins us, right?"

"Of course!" yelled Mrs. Bencourt, blushing. "Come on in and help yourself to the food, Kian!"

Friggin' terrific – he even had Teddy's mom walking a fine line with cougarhood. I wanted to scream and glared at Kian as he waved back to Mrs. Bencourt, a devastating smile on his perfect face.

The woman almost swooned.

I was going to barf.

Teddy looked him over. "So, I don't remember seeing you around. You new to the Cape?"

"I'm just visiting for the summer," replied Kian. "Ana has agreed to keep me entertained."

I flushed. "WHAT? I did NOT!"

Kian smiled in a cocky way that made me want to pinch him. Hard. "I'll grow on her . . . eventually."

on the pool deck, staring at the ocean beyond and the white sand beach.

"Think you could wait for me next time?" I asked, a little pissed I got dumped. Again. I never remembered girls being this slippery, although remembering back to my human days wasn't so easy after a century and a half.

MJ looked at me. "Why are you even here? You don't belong here."

"Why? Because I'm no longer in high school?"

Understatement of the year.

"Because you aren't a local," said Pix, turning toward me, her hands on her hips. "What are you, staying at a hotel?"

"Nope. I'm officially a 'local' as I bought my own place." I winked at her and her bowed mouth fell open in shock.

"You *what?*" asked MJ, his voice almost shrill. "What the frick do you mean you *bought a place?*"

I moved slowly, pretending to pull out my wallet and count cash. "I. Bought. A. Place. With. MONEY."

MJ muttered a few curses and stormed off toward the beach where a volleyball game was getting underway.

Pix was still staring at me. She blinked a few times. "You weren't kidding around, were you? You really are staying?"

I nodded, leaning against the railing that overhung the beach. "I said I was and I'm a man of my word. Are you mad?"

The way she looked at me, with such stunned innocence, sucked the wind out of my sails. She cleared her throat.

"I, uh, I'm just floored. I guess I'm not used to people, you know, following through on what they say they're going to do. Or what they promise."

"Perhaps the people you know suck?"

She laughed. "Or maybe I just bring out the worst in people."

"I doubt that, Pix. I think you bring out the best in me, and that's the truth. It's not a line and not a devious way to lure you to my bed."

She snorted.

"I'm serious!" I demanded with a laugh, standing up straighter and forcing her to step back. "I would like a chance to be a friend. You make me laugh and you challenge the hell out of me. It drives me insane."

She offered a crooked smile. "I may be just a bit competitive."

"Ya think?" I laughed, reaching out to tuck her windblown hair behind her shoulder, but she dodged my hand, and a moment of panic flushed her face.

Surprised at her reaction, I quickly dropped my hand. "Your hair was wrapping around your neck. I was just going to move it for you."

She looked a little mortified for a second, but recovered as she wrangled her hair behind her hoodie. "I can deal with my own hair, thanks."

I raised my hands in surrender. "Understood," I replied, but I found her reaction really odd. Not more than a day ago, we'd been dancing together, our bodies pressed to one another. But just now, it was almost as if, for a split second, she thought I was going to . . . hit her.

A cold fear started sinking through my gut.

I studied her carefully as she looked out over the beach at the volleyball game and to where MJ had parked himself in the sand by the sidelines. "Ana . . ."

She cut me off by flicking her head toward the white ball that was sailing back and forth over the net. "They never let MJ play – they think he's too tall and too skinny to play volleyball. They think he's just a big goofball and would be a liability."

She turned to me, her blue eyes blazing in the light from the bonfire below. "MJ and I aren't liabilities. We can hold our own, but no one ever gives us a chance to prove ourselves."

I leaned down on the railing studying the three people currently batting the ball over the net, recognizing one of them as Teddy. The other two I'd seen inside the house – another football player, who I heard a girl call *Jesse*, and a curvaceous brunette with an ice queen attitude.

"So how about we combine forces and kick the crap out of some volleyball players? Or can you not really play the game, Pix?"

A slow smile spread on her lips. "Oh, I can play, Key. I can totally play . . . and the carnage will be brutal."

22

I STOOD IN THE SHOWER at my house, a big, stupid grin on my face. I replayed the volleyball game in my mind over and over, happily setting the highlight reel to slo-mo for best effect. Kian, MJ and I annihilated Jesse, Teddy and Nikki Shea.

I would never forget the look on Nikki's face when Kian first ventured down to the net and asked if he could play. She was all, *"Oh YES . . . YOU can play with US,"* and then Kian corrected her, saying that MJ and I were his team.

Her face turned to stone.

While the game had started out as a friendly little battle, it quickly turned into full out war, attracting the attention of almost every kid at the party. It was a miracle that the ball actually survived all the smash hits and rage-fueled spikes.

MJ showed his unfailing accuracy, Kian's hits could drive the ball a foot into the sand, and I was a speed master with my shorter stature. None of us even noticed as the tide rose into our playing space and soon we were in ankle deep water, the net starting to sink.

We played like maniacs, smashing into the shallow water and chasing the slippery ball that was trying to escape with its leathery life. The crowd cheered, Nikki screamed, and Kian only pissed her off more.

We were the dream team.

We were epic.

It was one of the best nights of my life and I owed it to Kian and his one ridiculous idea of taking on those people who never saw me or MJ as valuable. When school started, many of the party-goers would still see me as the poverty-line mechanic whose mom apparently bailed for booze and pills, and whose dad was almost never around. But they'd also remember that I kicked ass at volleyball one summer night with the help of a goofy reject and a privileged washashore.

It was one more layer to my life that my classmates would have to deal with, though they'd no doubt try to write it off as a fluke.

Teddy, however, gave me a nod of approval when we won.

I finally finished rinsing out my hair and stepped out of the shower, wrapping myself in a towel as I opened the bathroom door.

I froze the moment I stepped into the hallway, startled at the sight of Dad sitting in front of the TV, staring at the blank screen, as if lost in thought. His jaw showed the beginnings of a beard from not shaving for the past few days while on the boat, and from my angle, he looked like a true sailor. A man bent into submission by the ocean and a life that showed little mercy.

He looked beat down by the world.

I took a cautious step forward, knowing he shouldn't be home. By the way he sat, I knew he didn't return early from a stellar haul of shellfish, but because of something else.

I took a quick breath, trying to scent the air for the smell of alcohol and scanned the room for a beer can or bottle. There was not a sign anywhere that he'd been drinking.

"Dad?" I asked carefully, clutching my towel as if the cotton could act as a shield.

He turned to look at me as a weary smile tried to show on his face. "Hey, Annie. Did you just get home?" he asked in that simple, roughened dad voice that used to read me stories – that dad voice that I clung to in my mind, before the booze took over.

God, he was sober.

More sober than I'd seen him in months.

I smiled, hopeful that maybe this would be a new beginning. That maybe this time I had a real chance of keeping him free of the beer and the vodka. "Uh, yeah. I was at Teddy Bencourt's place with MJ. He had a party and invited us."

Dad looked a little surprised, but not mad. He slid over and patted the worn couch cushion next to him. I slowly sat down beside him.

"The Bencourt's, huh? Did you have fun?" he asked.

I nodded, fighting back the emotion tightening my throat. My father was acting like the man I once knew, and I'd missed him desperately for so long. "I played volleyball and my team won."

"Good job, Girlie."

I swallowed. "Umm – why are you home? I mean, I'm happy you're here, but you said you wouldn't be back for a week. Is everything okay?" I was terrified of the answer. That whatever had driven him home early, would push him back to the liquor store.

He sighed. "*Charlotte* started having engine trouble. I had to bring her back in. Annie, I don't have the money to fix her. Mr. Waite has been patient with me, allowing me to slide on payments for his loan, but I can't ask him for more money. I've no clue what I'm gonna do."

"I can look at it," I chirped, a thrill of purpose launching me to my feet. I began calculating what tools I would need. I could do this for my dad. I could make him happy. That's all he needed to stay sober – he just needed to be happy.

I could fix this.

"It's not the same as a car engine, Annes," he argued.

"I can do it, Dad! I'll swing into the shop and grab what tools I think I'll need and head down to the harbor. You stay here and get some rest. Take a hot shower. I'll fix it, Dad – I promise. It'll be okay."

He smiled at me, but it lacked conviction. "It's almost midnight. You don't have to do it tonight. It can wait."

"No – I'm wide awake and it's a beautiful night. I'm wound up from the party anyway." I was actually flying high on the fact that my Dad was acting like his old self. It filled me with such excitement and hope that I'd never be able to sleep. I needed a job – this was the perfect solution.

I trotted into the kitchen and turned on the oven, pushing a frozen lasagna inside and setting the timer. "There! No arguments. I just put your dinner in the oven and I'll fix feisty *Charlotte*. You relax, get cleaned up and eat."

My dad slowly got to his feet and walked over to me, gathering me into his arms in a bear hug. His wind-burned hands scratched over my shoulders, and the smell of diesel and brine mixed on his clothes. He was branded, marked for life as man who sought the sea's bounty, day after day.

"I don't deserve such a good daughter as you, Ana."

I couldn't reply as I hugged him back, desperate not to cry. Finally he let me go and headed into the bathroom, and I quickly got dressed as I headed to fix his boat . . . and hopefully our lives.

23

KIAN

I SAT ON THE BOW of my new yacht, studying the darkened harbor that moved gently around me, wondering what Pix was up to.

Was she already asleep? Did she read before bed? Was she even IN her own bed or was she sleeping in her car once again?

After winning the volleyball game, I finally convinced her to give me her real phone number. She added it into my phone and I tested it by instantly calling her. It went through to her cell, assuring me I would not end up discussing wontons with a Chinese Take-Out joint if I rang.

The joy on her face, and that of MJ when we won, made me forget what I was. Made me suddenly become twenty years old once again, with hopes and dreams and the potential for a date with a certain dark-haired teammate.

A date. I was actually hoping for A DATE.

Hell, I didn't date. But Ana Lane made me human, and I desperately wanted to call her. To hear her voice on the other end of the line and pretend she was sitting with me on my boat, her feet tucked under her on the lounge, laughing at something I said.

I was turning into an idiot.

As I sat looking out over the water and the line of fishing boats that were tied up farther down the dock, I tried to clear my head. It was a gorgeous night, full of stars and a distant, fingernail moon. Pix would probably think it was nice, but typical Cape Cod, saying something like . . . crap. CRAP.

I was becoming addicted to Ana Lane! I literally couldn't get her out of my head!

Maybe hunting would help. Hunting HAD to help.

I began debating whether or not to head to Sandy Neck and raid the deer population, when I saw headlights swing into the lot near the fishing boats. Even in the darkness, I could easily make out a familiar rolling hunk of junk, and my heart actually sped up.

I quickly got to my feet, heading to the yacht's railing to get a better view of Pix as she stepped out of her car wearing – lord, have mercy – ultra short cutoffs and a black tank top. She wandered to the back of her car and opened the trunk, hauling out two tool boxes.

Slamming the trunk shut, she headed for one of the commercial boats, sliding the tools onto the deck before she climbed aboard. Then she disappeared below deck.

Fate obviously wanted me to see her.

Who was I to fight destiny?

At least, that was the excuse I was going with as I made my way down onto the docks and headed to a battered fishing boat named *Miss Charlotte*.

I carefully climbed aboard and listened as the Foo Fighters' music drifted up from below deck. I could hear Pix's voice singing along and the sound of metal hitting metal.

She was working . . . and in a great mood.

I silently made my way below deck and immediately saw Pix in a hole in the floor of the kitchen galley, working on a grease-ridden engine. Between the music and her focus, she was oblivious to my presence and I watched her work, free for once to enjoy her as she really was – without her defensive armor or sharp wit aimed at my manhood.

Sweat was beginning to form on her neck from the effort of working at the engine's stubborn parts, and she leaned back slightly as she wrangled her hair into a pony tail over her tank top, not caring that grease streaked her hair and tinted her skin.

She went back to work, continuing to sing, but then something shifted on the engine and she cursed in pain.

I moved instantly to help her and she nearly smacked me in the head with a wrench. "HOLY HELL!" she screamed. "What are you doing here? You ARE A STALKER! MJ WAS RIGHT!"

"Calm down, will you!" I urged as I grabbed hold of the heavy engine part that had slid sideways onto her foot, and lifted it away. She managed to pull her foot out and I set the part back down with a *clang*. I could hear her heart hammering, whether from me scaring her or her foot, I was unsure. I looped one arm under her legs and the other behind her back and she tensed.

"What are you doing?" she demanded.

"I'm lifting you out of this hole so I can get your sneaker off and see how bad your foot is, so calm down." Not waiting for an argument, I lifted her into the small kitchen area of the fishing boat and then sat back next to her on the floor.

She glared at me. "Why are you following me?"

"I'm not. I bought a yacht and it's docked here at the harbor. I saw your car pull in and thought I'd surprise you, but before I could say anything, you broke somebody's engine."

"I didn't break it, wise ass. I'm trying to fix it. This is my dad's boat," she replied. "And since when do you like boats? You looked as though you were gonna toss your cookies on the ferry, and now you're living on a yacht?"

"I already told you, I wasn't seasick on the ferry – it just smelled like mold and tourists." I smiled back, but then saw her wince as she shifted her leg. "I really should take a look at your foot. That piece of the engine is really heavy."

"No kidding? Wanna tell me how you managed to lift it, Hercules?"

Shit. "Uh – adrenaline. People can do amazing things when adrenaline kicks in. I'm sure I'll feel it in a few hours." I flexed my shoulder, rubbing it as if I were already feeling some pain, which was total BS.

She eyed me suspiciously. "Whatever. And I'm sure I'll be fine. I don't need you to play doctor," she argued trying to get to her feet. She sucked in a tight breath when her foot made contact with the floor, and I grabbed her before she fell on her face.

In my arms she felt soft and warm and . . . tempting.

"Damn it, I need to finish this!" she yelled, squirming as she pointed to the engine. "Just put me back down there and I'll deal with my foot later! I've got to fix this!"

She was so pissed off and feisty, that I would've been entirely turned on if it weren't for the fact that I knew she was hurting. "Pix, you obviously can't do anything in pain. Let me bring you back to my yacht for a bit and check on your foot. If we're lucky, it's just bruised and we can ice it. Get off it for an hour or so, and see if it gets better."

She stood there, staring at the engine that looked like a jigsaw puzzle, totally defeated. I couldn't let her drag herself back down there without making sure she hadn't broken her foot.

"I'll tell you what, Pix – let me take you to my place and rest that foot and then, when you want to come back to Titanic here, I'll accompany you and be your helper. You tell me what to do and where, and together we'll make up for the lost time you seem so concerned about."

She looked up at me and the smallest smile flashed on her face. "So, you'll be my minion, eh?"

"I'll be whatever you need me to be," I replied in a husky, teasing voice, which earned me a hard pinch from my semi-date.

24

ANA

As LOUSY LUCK WOULD have it, I couldn't even put weight on my stupid foot, so Kian offered to carry me to his yacht. Refusing to be a total damsel in distress, I only agreed to a piggyback ride. Thank god no one else was around to see me, greasy and disheveled, hitching a ride on the back of a gorgeous yacht owner.

As he walked along the docks with me clinging to his back, his arms holding my legs, I was floored at how solid he felt under me. It was entirely possible that he had zero fat on his perfect body, which was – HELLO – intimidating.

"So, why are you out here in the middle of the night working on your dad's boat? Couldn't it have waited until morning?" he asked, his voice vibrating through his back.

Kian's words brought back a vision of my dad looking so defeated on our old couch and how determined I was to make him feel better. To make him see that life could be better despite our rotten luck. "My dad just needs me to fix it. That's all. And I couldn't sleep, so I came down here.

Even if I'd waited until morning, I would've just obsessed about it all night."

I could feel Kian take a deep breath. "You really are selfless, Pix. I admire that in you, but I also hope you put yourself first every once in a while."

"Technically fixing the engine will make *me* feel better – I WANT to do it, so I guess, in some ways, it is selfish," I argued.

"If everyone subscribed to your version of 'selfish' the world would be a much better place," replied Kian, slowing at the stern of a massive, ruby-hulled yacht. I clutched him tighter as he stepped off the dock onto the boat's dive deck and made his way up the stairs, which were carved into the stern. He finally set me down on a white lounge on the aft deck.

I looked around at the stunning boat, taking in its beautiful dark tones of burgundy and teak. "Good grief, what did you do – buy this off the Rat Pack?"

"Nope – I didn't buy this off a Hollywood star. At least, I don't think I did. I bought it at auction," replied Kian, sitting down on an ottoman by my feet and carefully raising my leg so my foot sat in his lap. The parts of me that were so close to parts of him, made me all shivery inside.

I nervously watched as he slowly untied my dirty shoelaces, and I became acutely aware of how pristine the yacht was versus how grubby I was. "I really shouldn't be on your boat. I'm going to get it filthy. I mean – for Pete's sake,

I'm going to leave a mark on this freakin' white sofa! Just sit me on the floor or something."

Kian continued to untie my shoe and just smiled. "I'm not putting you on the floor, Pix. And I'm not worried about the furniture – that's why maids were invented." He carefully took hold of my leg in one hand, his palm warming a perfect circle on my calf as he eased the sneaker off.

I dug my fingers into my thighs as pain shot through the side of my foot. Kian's eyes darted to mine for a second, gauging my level of agony. I bit my lip as he finally got the shoe off and started on my sock. "You doing okay?" he asked, hesitating.

"Yup." I managed to bite out. "Just get the damn thing off."

He finally pulled the sock off, revealing my now Halloween-worthy foot, which was swollen on the top and to the side. It was getting red, no doubt destined to be some nasty black and purple tone by dawn.

I knew how bruises worked on my skin – I'd had enough of them over the years to know exactly how long they took to appear and how best to hide them.

Kian grabbed a pillow from the opposite lounge and propped my foot on it, then headed inside the yacht to get some ice.

Finally alone, I leaned back against the lounge and looked up to the sky, admiring the wealth of stars that seemed to expand deep into the universe. On nights like this, I felt as though I could see through time – through every constellation and uncharted world that might exist beyond our own.

Dad used to say that the night sky was truly endless when you were out at sea. He said that when the water was dead calm, and the moon was hiding beneath the curve of earth, it felt as though he was actually floating in space. On the blackest of nights, he said you couldn't see where the ocean stopped and the universe began and suddenly you were one with the stars. On those nights, you became your own constellation and a mere speck in a galaxy so vast, that no one else existed.

Sometimes I wished that my father and I could escape into that kind of endless night. It would be a spot wedged between the sea and sky, where the burdens and demons of the past couldn't find us – a place where we were finally at peace with the world and one another.

I realized then that I DID feel that peace, but not with my dad. Not even with MJ. I felt it with . . . Kian.

I snapped out of my shocking revelation when I heard him return. He sat back down in front of me and I reached for the towel-wrapped ice he had in his hand, but he lifted it out of my grabby fingers.

"Relax, Pix. I can do it," he said, placing my foot carefully back on his lap.

How was it even possible I enjoyed this guy's company? He was everything I always avoided and yet I liked being around him.

"Well, I can do it too. I don't need you to baby me," I protested, but the contrast of the heat from his hands and the coolness of the ice pack felt fantastic.

Kian studied me carefully, his blue eyes seeming to read through all my lies and defenses.

He eased the ice pack slightly, moving it to another part of my foot as he watched me. "I get the sense that you are used to taking care of yourself *and* everyone else. Who exactly takes care of you, though?"

"I don't need someone taking care of me. I do just fine taking care of myself, thanks very much." The discussion was making me uneasy, especially since I still couldn't get a read on Kian's emotions. Being forced to decipher his body language, just like everyone else, sucked.

With Kian O'Reilly, my emotional barometer failed to work, and it made me feel exposed in his presence. Perhaps the fact that he was such a mystery was the reason WHY I liked him.

The silence between us stretched, made even louder by the quiet echo of the ropes straining to hold the yacht in place against the receding tide. The temperature had begun to drop and I rubbed my arms, trying to chase away the goosebumps.

Kian, never one to miss a damn thing, noticed.

"Let's go inside. The yacht is warm and I can make you something to drink. And don't protest for once. Please? It's late."

Rather than wait for an answer, he eased my foot down and came over to me, picking me up in a cradle hold. I went to protest his stupid chivalry, but he shot me a look that sealed my lips.

We headed into the yacht's main glassed-in parlor and the subtle warmth of the area felt wonderful. He set me down on another couch and handed me a fuzzy red throw and the ice pack, then wandered over to a full bar.

I rested the ice over my foot, which was feeling a little better thanks to the cold. I, however, was getting tired. The clock near the bar showed it to be after one in the morning. If I'd kept going on the engine, I could've powered past any sleepiness, but sitting around and being pampered was getting to me.

I stifled a yawn.

"I have peppermint hot cocoa or double chocolate," Kian announced, pulling a mug from the cabinet.

"Either. Thanks," I said, trying to perk myself up. How does anyone have such a comfy couch on a boat? It was better than my bed, for crying out loud!

I needed to keep talking. Stay awake.

"So, why a yacht?" I asked, trying to avoid another yawn.

"Well, I like to travel. And my family, historically, were boat builders. It made sense to have a place that I could take with me wherever I went. And this has all the comforts of a nice home – two bedrooms, a modern kitchen, and a nice bathroom are all below us."

He walked across the parlor with a steaming cup of chocolate goodness and handed it to me. I blew over the swirling, milky top and took a sip. It was insane. "Dang, this is good," I breathed.

Kian sat down near me in an armchair, smiling. "Thanks. I got it at a local shop called the Chocolate Raven. They make custom blends of cocoa."

"I didn't know you liked hot chocolate," I replied, silently wondering why he didn't have any in his own hand.

"I don't, but you seemed to enjoy the one I bought you on the ferry. I figured I better stock some here on the boat – you know, for any friends that might swing by." He smiled brilliantly at me and leaned forward, shifting the ice pack again and checking my foot.

I was too stunned to reply.

He looked up and saw that I was staring at him. "It's not a bad thing to have someone putting your needs first once in a while, Pix. I see how hard you work and you, above anyone else I've ever known, deserve that."

I couldn't meet his eyes any longer and looked down to my drink. "Thanks," I mumbled, but then my mutinous body forced out another yawn. "Crap. I need to wake up. I can't fall asleep here."

"Why not?" asked Kian. "I have plenty of space and I swear, I'll be on my best behavior." He made a little cross over his heart and put two fingers up. "Scout's honor."

"You were NOT a Boy Scout. No way they would've accepted your cocky butt. Total liar, you are."

Kian dropped his salute. "Okay – that's true, but I swear to be a total, boring pal. Nothing more. And we can get up at the butt crack of dawn and start hammering away at that antique engine of your dad's."

"I still need to put away all my tools – someone could steal them. And I need to lock up my car," I argued, though the couch felt more and more comfortable by the second.

Dumb piece of intoxicating furniture.

Kian stood, pulling the blanket over me more and tucking in the edges so I couldn't wiggle out. "I'll go get your tools, but I'm leaving your car unlocked."

"WHAT? WHY!" I demanded.

"Because hopefully someone is dumb enough to steal that piece of crap," he laughed.

"Lock the car!" I ordered, wriggling my arms free. "It's not even mine! It belongs to Jack and the shop."

Kian headed for the door, but turned to look back at me on his couch, a grin on his face. "I'm sure Jack would love to see that thing stolen too. Maybe I should just torch it?"

"KIAN!" I yelled, and then chucked a throw pillow at my snide rescuer, who easily dodged my aim.

25

KIAN

TWENTY MINUTES LATER, I had done as instructed, but resisted the urge to shift her crappy car into neutral and shove it off the boat launch. When I returned to the yacht, I found her asleep in the same spot I'd left her.

Carefully, I removed the ice pack from her foot, which now was displaying the beginnings of an angry bruise. I softly placed my hand on the injury, careful not to wake her.

Focusing on what I wanted, I called forward the life forces that were naturally stored in my body from my victims. In response, the Fallen Marks began to bloom on my skin, swirling and twisting over my face and body and traveling down my arms and over my hands.

Ever so carefully, I set to healing Ana's foot, using a filtered form of the power from the souls I'd stolen. My marks extended lightly onto her skin, healing her gently.

While I was probably making her foot tingle, she was too dead asleep to be bothered by what I was doing. Even better, she was merely bruised, and thus she would barely feel anything while I worked. A more severe injury, however, could be painful when repaired.

I looked at Ana's peaceful face, and couldn't get past the sense that I was missing something so obvious about her life. Something that drove her to be so fierce and defiant. I suspected she placed her faith in very few people, and yet she slept soundly in my home.

I realized then that she actually trusted me. Believed that I was *safe*. I was many things, but *safe* had never been one of them, especially around humans. The understanding of what it probably took for Ana Lane to be brave enough to trust me, hit me like a steel bat to the chest.

I drew my hands away, shaken by my revelation.

The area of her foot that had been injured was now blemish free and perfect. Sleeping soundly on my couch, *she* looked perfect . . . and very breakable.

God, what was I doing?

If she ever found out that I'd kept the body of a man I had killed in the back of the Auburn, she'd never speak to me again. Actually, the instant she found out what I really was, she would hate me for all time.

And one thing that would absolutely break me, would be to know that Ana Lane hated me.

26

 ANA

CERTAIN THINGS SHOULD BE TOTALLY ILLEGAL.

Allowing Kian O'Reilly to go anywhere shirtless with his damp hair slicked back, would top that list.

Seeing him leaning against the bar in the early morning light with his golden skin and perfect six-pack of abs on display, was like texting and driving at a high rate of speed. Trying to peel my eyes off of him was nearly impossible and had I been walking, I would've smacked into a wall. Thank goodness I was sneaking a nice, long peek at him from my cozy spot on the couch.

I watched him as he slowly turned the page of a newspaper he was reading, smoothing out the edges. When it crinkled under his touch, he glanced up to me, no doubt to see if he'd disturbed me.

When he caught me watching him, he pushed aside the paper with a smile that rivaled the freakin' sun. "You're awake."

"You're observant," I muttered, pissed that I was getting all hot and bothered by the mere sight of a smoking hot guy.

I wondered if he smelled as good as he looked?

Oh my god. I needed to get a grip!

"I see that you wake up on the ultra-friendly side of the bed in the morning. Good to know," he replied, coming around the bar and – damn it – he NEEDED a belt!

With his sweatpants riding WAY too low and showing off every perfectly carved muscle on his torso, I couldn't think straight.

Face. I needed to look at his FACE.

He sat down across from me, offering me a wide mug of coffee. "How'd you sleep?" he asked as I slid up more, bringing my legs toward my chest. I glanced down at my foot and was surprised to see that the ice had worked phenomenally well – no bruise and no pain.

I accepted the mug from him and took a sip, humming my approval. "Good. Like a rock, actually. What time is it?"

He rested his elbows on his thighs, watching me. "Around six. I'm assuming you want to get back to work on your dad's boat?"

I nodded. "He needs her up and running as soon as possible. Did you grab all the tools?"

"I did and don't worry – I locked up your excuse of an automobile. It's probably still out in the lot, since not even the chop shop would want that thing."

"Ha ha. Don't knock my ride, Key. Free is free, that's all I know," I argued, pushing the warm blanket aside and getting to my feet. Kian stood with me, watching me carefully, as if I was going to keel over.

"How's the foot?" he asked.

"Better. Perfect. Ice works wonders."

He smiled, "Yes it does. Works like magic."

* * * *

It took nearly three hours to fix *Charlotte* and by the time we were finished, all I wanted to do was dive into the harbor and cool off. Kian, however, didn't even break a sweat.

Typical.

"So – shall we take her out for a test drive and make sure your brilliant mechanical skills are really as great as you think they are?" he asked, wiping the grease from his hands with a rag.

He had followed every order I'd given him all morning, never questioning what I was doing. Quite frankly, his willingness to just do as I asked, floored me. I'd never, EVER, had a guy blindly follow orders from me when I worked on a car. Not Jack, not Teddy, and definitely not Corbin.

But Kian? He trusted my skills entirely, and that made him a rare soul in my book.

"Sure. I'll just let the harbormaster know I'm not stealing it," I laughed, heading to the office. On my way back, however, I saw Kian talking on his phone. He looked at me coming and waved me over, holding the phone out to me.

I gave him a confused look.

"It's MJ," he said as I took the phone. "He's been trying to get a hold of you all night. He ended up calling me, trying to find you."

I took the phone. "MJ? What's the matter? What's happened?"

"Where the hell are you? I drove by your house and your dad's truck is in the driveway! I've been freaking out, trying to find you all night. I worried that something happened between the two of you. Are you okay? Did you know he's home?"

I glanced at Kian who was watching me with concern. He mouthed the words, *everything okay?* and I nodded, waving him off as I walked down the dock. I didn't want him to overhear any of the conversation.

"I'm so sorry, MJ. I should've called. Yeah – I know he's back. He wasn't supposed to be back for another few days, but *Charlotte* was having engine problems. I just fixed her this morning with Kian's help."

The phone went silent for a moment. *"You could've called me. I would've helped you with Miss Charlotte."*

Okay, now I felt very guilty. "Don't worry about it. I actually came to the harbor alone last night – really late. I was working on the boat when Kian showed up. He has a yacht on the docks. That's what he bought – that's the place he was talking about."

"So then where did you sleep all night? On Charlotte?" asked MJ slowly.

"Well, I was planning to. I could've gone home too, because Dad was fine. I mean, REALLY okay – for like the first time in forever."

"Ana . . ."

"Don't. Don't say it. This time will be different. I can feel it – I can sense my dad's desire to be better. I can FEEL his hopefulness trying to come forward. Everything is going to be better," I replied, looking back at Kian who was talking to one of the dock workers, but glancing at me now and then.

"Please be careful – with your dad and with Kian. I don't trust either of them and I'd lose my mind if something happened to you. Honestly, I'm surprised you are hanging out with a guy like Kian. I mean, you must be reading him, knowing exactly what type of womanizer he probably is."

I paused, debating whether or not to tell MJ that I actually *couldn't* read Kian. "I'm a big girl. I know who he is and we're just friends. Remember - you too had a good time with him at Teddy's party. Give him a chance, MJ."

I heard my dear friend sigh. *"Fine. Do you want to hit the waves at Cahoon's Hollow tonight? OH! And I got a Matt Kechele board from the Boarding House Surf Shop. I thought you might want to give her a try."*

I blinked, floored. MJ had managed to score a slice of fiberglass perfection that I'd only ridden in my dreams. The envy I was feeling was acute. "A Kechele Sprocket? Are you kidding me? HECK YES!"

"And . . . I guess you can bring Boat Boy along."

I squealed in the phone, causing MJ to curse. "I LOVE you! You are the bestest bestie eva!"

"Oh my god, don't scream in my ear, woman! I'll see you down there around five," he replied with a small laugh. *"Bye."*

"BYE!" I hooted, jumping around as I hung up. I skipped my way back to *Miss Charlotte* where Kian was standing by one of the pylons wrapped with barge rope.

"Did you really squeal a second ago? Because I didn't peg you for a squealer," asked Kian, a smirk on his face.

"I did NOT squeal. I may have yelled in a semi-squeaky voice, but it wasn't a squeal. Plus, MJ invited us to go surfing this afternoon. You down for hanging ten at Cahoons Hollow around five tonight?"

"You totally squealed – like a GIRL, I might add. And yes – I'm always down for surfing. Now, shall we take this ancient, seafaring vessel for a cruise around the harbor or what?"

I nodded, thrilled and hopeful that life was suddenly smiling on me. Maybe I no longer had to worry so much about making it to eighteen and escaping my life.

Maybe, for once, I had a chance to really live.

PART 2

TRUTHS

27

KIAN

AS I PULLED THE CORVETTE into the packed parking lot of the Milk Way, I was stunned to realize I had known Ana for nearly a month.

The summer felt as though it were flying by, and I knew I owed it all to her. She brought me so close to my human self that I sometimes forgot I was a killer. She was blurring the lines between my reality and my fantasy and it made me feel like I never had before.

After helping her on her father's boat three weeks ago and surfing with her and MJ, I was careful to give her space and only call her occasionally. Soon, however, I found that it was SHE who began to call ME.

At first her calls were for more business-like things, like upcoming car shows and places that I should see while I was visiting. What she didn't know was that I intended to stay far longer than the summer. She'd become my mission in life – a driving force to be better, to be more selfless.

At least, that's what I kept telling myself.

158

Deep down, however, I was stupidly falling in love with her, and I knew it. For a million reasons, getting involved with a human was a terrible idea. I'd known only a few soul thieves who had managed to form relationships with humans, but they always ended and often not in the human's favor.

Of course, if I was *truly* dedicated to being selfless, I would've left, ensuring our friendship would never extend farther than a few friendly phone calls. But I wasn't leaving because I wanted her in my life, and being selfish was far easier. Being selfish suited me just fine.

As our calls became more frequent, she began inviting me to do things with her that had nothing to do with my status as "car-buying washashore." We began surfing constantly together. I saw my very first drive-in movie with her in Wellfleet. We got to check out the car museum in Sandwich, and the live music on the Village Green in Hyannis. I even helped her work on her Trans Am, which, weirdly, I found satisfying.

Who knew blue collared slavery could be so fulfilling?

She even named the yacht after some dog from Harry Potter called *Cerberus*, though MJ did point out that Cerberus was technically called *Fluffy* in the book. I voted THAT name down instantly.

We began taking *Cerberus* out for day trips to Martha's Vineyard, especially when Ana would need to work at Waite's house. While she was there, I'd stake out the house from a distance because, quite frankly, something just felt off about the whole situation.

I couldn't understand *why* a businessman would have a teenager (and the daughter of one of his borrowers), work in his garage. That screamed "conflict of interest" to me, or at the very least, a lawsuit waiting to happen. Businessmen as savvy as Waite wouldn't make such a mistake.

Thank god Pix didn't go there often, though I wanted to convince her to stop working for that recluse. If I brought up my concerns, however, I knew she'd see it as a controlling maneuver, and that I may really be the overbearing, entitled brat that she thought I was initially.

I suspected that she was always looking for a sign that I wasn't the flawless, kindhearted, loaded guy that I was trying to be. It kept me on my toes and on a strict diet of animal souls.

Not wanting to alarm the park rangers with a creepy amount of dead deer, I tried to spread out my hunting grounds north and west of the Cape, though I did try hunting seal once.

It was an unwise choice.

Seals bite. Hard. They are also slippery and rubbery and for being porkers, they can haul ass when they want to. Plus those bastards harbor grudges – a fact I found out when I went back a second time and was chased across the sand by about 20 spotted buggers roaring at me.

Animals almost always steer clear of Mortis, so suddenly being chased by a herd of angry pinnipeds was a shock. After that night, I vowed to stay with deer, dogs, and coywolves, all of which were far safer than seals.

I wish I could share those things with Ana and be completely honest with her. I wish I could let her see the true me, and I was certain she'd be delighted to know I had to outrun a mob of angry blubber.

As I stepped from my car and walked towards the shop, I began to daydream about her listening to my stories and confessions. In my mind, I saw her accepting me for all the faults and horrible things I'd done in my life.

In my mind, she told me it was okay.

In my mind, she kissed me.

I slowed as I approached the door to the busy shop, calming my roaring imagination, but then I heard Pix's voice. It was coming from the backside of the building, and I slowly eased my way along the weathered shingles, listening.

She was engaged in a heated discussion out behind one of the freezers with Apron Boy, both semi-hiding at the rear of the building.

"He's gonna have setbacks!" she snapped in a low tone. "He was good for almost a full three weeks! He'll get back on track. I know he will! And this was my fault. I got in his way."

The anger in MJ's response was damn near palpable.

"THIS is not EVER your fault. Damn it! Don't do this to yourself again. Don't get your hopes up and let your guard down. You have a plan, Ana. Stick to it. And don't, DON'T, be home when he is."

"He can't be helped if I'm not keeping an eye on him when he's home. He wants to get better. He just needs me there, keeping him focused."

"HE DOES NOT WANT TO BE SAVED! It's not your job to fix him!" yelled MJ, whose sharp tone made me unwilling to lurk any longer. I stepped around the side of the building and Ana saw me out of the corner of her eye, quickly turning away.

"Go away, Kian!" she demanded, startled.

"What's going on?" I asked carefully, looking between Ana's turned back and MJ, who was rubbing his face in frustration.

"Make him leave, MJ. Please," she whispered, but MJ just shook his head.

Good grief, had I done something wrong?

MJ, who was still not a fan of mine, looked at me with a hardened gaze. "I can't hide this much longer and she won't listen to me. And while I don't like you, I'm hoping she will listen to you."

He turned back to Ana, who still refused to look at me. "Ana, this can't continue and somewhere deep down, you know I'm right. Maybe Kian can make you see reason, because the mirror obviously can't."

I watched as he walked away, leaving the two of us alone at the back of the shop. I stepped over to where Pix stood, her back to me and her hair shielding her face.

"What's going on?" I asked carefully.

"I'm fine. I can handle it. MJ is just freaking out, as usual. It'll all be fine." She reached out and picked at the peeling paint on one of the cedar shingles and it floated to the ground, planting itself among a bunch of flowering weeds.

Rather than ask her to turn to me, I stepped around in front of her and she tensed, trying to hide her face again, but this time I saw it – the remnants of true violence.

Rage lit to life in my chest as I sucked in a sharp curse. "Who did this to you?" I asked, barely maintaining my sanity. A dozen ways in which to murder an asshole ran through my head at warp speed.

I liked them all.

Ana gave up on hiding and turned toward me, fully displaying a bruised cheek and swollen lip. Someone had dared to turn their anger on her and left a reminder of their selfishness on her fair skin. Whoever it was, had one day left to their miserable life, I'd make sure of it.

Ana crossed her arms and looked at me, determination in her eyes. "It was an accident and it's not that big of a deal."

"Like HELL it's not a big deal." I snapped, causing her to startle.

I needed to calm down.

The last thing she needed was for me to turn into a fuming maniac in front of her. I tried again, controlling my need to put my fist through the wall. "Pix – it's a big deal. People don't accidentally hit other people in the face. Who did this to you?" *So I can rip his arms off and beat him senseless with his own hands.*

She shook her head, refusing to talk. This was why MJ was loosing his cool – she was protecting someone, or she was keeping silent out of fear. Either way, I was determined to find out who had abused her and give him a lesson in real torture.

I took a deep breath. "It's okay if you don't want to tell me, but I'm not leaving you here. I want to make sure your cheek bone isn't . . . broken."

Okay, now I actually felt sick from the rampant flow of hate flying through my veins.

She shook her head. "I can't go with you – I need to get to work. I'll just work out back, but Jack expects me to be there. He'll be mad if I don't show up."

Mad? As in pissed enough to strike a female employee? Or maybe it was that moron, Corbin. Or that kid, Teddy. Hell, it could even be an ex-boyfriend that she was having issues with.

But then something occurred to me: she slept in the car. She'd slept in the car the first night I met her. MJ spoke as if she was trying to help someone. Dear god, was this not the first time she'd been beaten? Did it have to do with her home life?

"I'll call Jack. I'll tell him you fell off your bike or something. You need a few days off."

She began to protest, but I reached out to her and softly touched her chin. "Pix, right now it doesn't look like an accident and it's pretty bad. I get the sense you don't want people to know, and if you go to work, it'll be very obvious something is going on. Jack will probably call the police, unless . . . did Jack do this?"

She snorted. "Of course not."

"Do you want him to know? Because if you go to work, he WILL know, and he will definitely call the police. I'd like to call the police as well, but I think you don't want me to and I'll honor that, as long as you come back to *Cerberus* with me."

Actually, I would never call the police.

I'd just dole out my own form of irrevocable justice.

Ana examined the ground, studying the weeds that clung to her lonely paint chip. She finally nodded and looked towards my car that was all the way across the parking lot.

"Fine, I'll go with you. But would you mind bringing the corvette over here? I don't wanna scare away the patrons with my zombie face," she said, trying to make light of a terrible wrong.

She gave me a small smile, forcing her bruise to twist, contorting her swollen lip. With her face a sharp contrast of hope and hell, acceptance and defiance, she finally let me in, and I silently swore a fierce oath to protect her.

28

M WAS RIGHT — I'D LET MY guard down. I'd become lulled by hope into a false sense of security and believed that my dad had finally shaken his demons.

It was the longest I'd seen him sober — nearly three full weeks. He was different, more like his old self, though he did seem down. I thought he was just fatigued. I thought money weighed on him.

I worked more hours at the shop and at Mr. Waite's, hoping the extra cash would ease his sadness, but it didn't seem to make a dent.

I should've noticed what he was going through, but I was with Kian, and Kian made me *different*.

Made me live . . . for me.

Looking back, I realized that Dad wasn't sleeping well. He didn't eat well. When he was home, he would talk to me, but never about anything of critical importance and I didn't care. He was at least talking to me, even if it was simply about the weather or the latest haul of scallops, and it made me feel connected to him once again. To me, it was a scrap of hope that I clung to desperately, praying it would strengthen with time.

I stopped sleeping in my car when he was home and, after a few days, stopped locking my bedroom door.

That was a terrible mistake.

I don't know what exactly broke his will to stay sober, though I suspected it had to do with money. Or work. It was always money or work or both, but he must've seen the light under my bedroom door late at night. That must've been what pushed him over the edge.

I'd been up reading, trying to calm down after spending the evening with Kian. I'd been rerunning the fantastic time we'd had surfing, daring one another to try different tricks on the boards he'd bought. At one point I got rolled pretty badly and he managed to haul me back up to the surface and out of the rip current.

He actually looked a little panicked as I laid on my board, coughing and laughing as I tried to catch my breath. No one ever looked worried for me, except for MJ . . . but MJ didn't cause the weird twist to my stomach like Kian did.

MJ didn't slip into my dreams at night and whisper things to me that I never even longed for before. Things I now craved, but only with Kian.

But now Kian would forever see me as someone to pity. He'd see me as someone who was a coward and totally broken. He'd see my hope as pointless and my life as a tangled disaster. God, I would give anything to get the last twelve hours back and do things differently. Do things like I should've.

I should've left the light off and used my flashlight to read. I should've locked the door. I should've slept in the car. I should've done a lot of things, but I'd let my guard down and I couldn't go back and do it right. History can't be rewritten, no matter how much we beg time for a do over.

Quite honestly, I deserved the beating I got because I was the one who was careless and I knew lights cost money.

"Stop trying to find the logic in it," said Kian quietly as he drove us to the docks. He'd been pensively silent while he drove, daring a stolen glance at my damaged face now and then.

"I'm not," I replied, a total lie.

"I think I know you well enough that I'm sure you're trying to take the blame for this, and I won't let you do that to yourself. Do you hear me? Whoever struck you, should be shot!"

"He doesn't deserve to be shot!" I snapped back, beginning to lose my cool. "He just needs help and he doesn't mean to do it. Sometimes he doesn't even remember, damn it. It's not a big deal."

I could see all the muscles in Kian's arms flex as he drove, a sure sign he was barely keeping his anger under control. He didn't talk to me for the remainder of the ride to the harbor, and while I knew he wanted to strangle the man who hurt me, I also knew he thought I was an idiot.

Kian pulled his car into the parking spot next to *Cerberus'* dock and cut the engine. We sat there, looking out the window at the beautiful yacht and the sailboats cruising by.

I sighed. "I get it. You think I'm stupid for standing up for him. Heck, if I was you, I'd say I deserve what I got for sticking up for him."

Kian turned to me sharply. "Good god, I don't think you're stupid. I think you're brave and determined and you think you can fix anything. But Pix, some things – some people – are unfixable. People need to WANT to change, and the person who has done this . . ." He reached out and carefully turned my jaw to see the full extent of the damage to my face. "The person who did *this* doesn't want to change."

I gently grasped his wrist and pulled his hand away from my face. "He does want to change. I can *feel* it."

"Pix . . ." Kian shook his head.

"No! I KNOW he wants to change. I can read his emotion – his true want. He wants to get better. And I stay because I can also read his love for me when he isn't out of control and he's himself. I can feel he loves me."

I swallowed, and Kian watched me closely as I raised a hand to his face and traced his temple, touching the soft edges of his blond hair. "I can't read you, though. You are an unknown to me, like an abyss that holds onto its secrets. I feel blind when I'm with you."

"You are . . . psychic?" he asked, curious, and I shook my head. I was surprised he didn't think I was nuts.

"No. It's more like getting a strong read off of someone's emotions and desires. It's not that fancy to be honest. I can't, like, read minds or anything."

Kian leaned towards me, and suddenly the car felt far smaller than it already was. His gaze traveled from my eyes to my lips and back again and I thought I might be having some sort of mental short circuit. The fact that my heart was hammering in my ears wasn't helping either.

"So, you can't read what I really want?" he asked, a tone that seemed deeper and smoother somehow lacing his words.

I gave the smallest shake of my head.

He studied me for a moment as he slid his thumb softly over my swollen lip. He seemed to be caught in his own, internal discussion and I watched him, a mix of curiosity and desperate *want* spinning inside me like the cotton candy machine at the fair.

"Stay with me," he finally whispered. "I know that you slept in your car the first night I met you and I know that you avoid your house. You told me that it's only you and your father at home." His brow wrinkled in anger. "Is it your father? Did he strike you?

I refused to give voice to the obvious and simply kept my eyes on his, staying silent. If I didn't say it out loud, I could still fix it and move on with life, burying the past. I could pretend the years of abuse were just a distant mistake of my father's.

Kian sighed, "Stay here, on *Cerberus*, with me. You no longer need to sleep in the car, Ana. Stay here, where you are safe and can sleep without fear."

I looked out the window at *Cerberus*, her candied apple hull a sharp contrast to the dark blue water flexing under her. Here I was, being offered a chance at freedom from worry – to live a life of perfection with a stunning guy who seemed to worry over me.

Unfortunately it felt like pity, and I didn't do well with pity. Or charity. If I were going to stay, I'd pay my way.

"I'll stay, but only when my dad is home. And I'll pay rent," I replied.

"Uh, no. I'm not taking your money. Screw that," he replied, leaning back against his side of the car, a look of humor on his face.

"Well, I sure ain't paying you in *other* ways," I replied, trying to act insulted though I knew Kian wouldn't take me up as a rejected form of Vivian Ward.

At least . . . I didn't think he would.

Damn, I wish I could read the bugger. Watch him be related to that chick in that book with the vampires . . .

"Pix, I don't trade in those forms of payment. Ever. Nor do I want you to think that anyone has the right to ask you to trade your body in exchange for help. A girl – woman – like you, deserves to be worshiped. She should be adored and her body should be respected and revered. If any guy ever offers you less, kick him to the curb and back the Trans Am over him. Twice."

With that, Kian stepped out of his side of the car, leaving my head spinning. Where did this guy come from? Hell, was he even HUMAN?

As he opened the door for me, I couldn't help but believe in a higher power, because Kian O'Reilly was one rebellious, rock star of an angel.

And I was entirely falling for him.

29

KIAN

ANA KNEW THE LAYOUT of the yacht like the back of her hand. We had hung out here a few times and I'd been smart enough to start having the local grocer deliver to the yacht because of her visits (and bring with him lots of chocolate, which Pix was a mad fan of). I hoped her familiarity with *Cerberus* made it feel like a welcoming place for her to let her guard down.

As soon as we'd gotten onboard, Ana asked if she could take a shower, so I laid out a set of new towels in the bathroom for her. I was grateful that I'd bought her a RoxyBlue t-shirt and lounge pants a few weeks back when I'd gotten my surfboards, and I gave them to her as she stood in the bathroom. She was shocked, but grateful.

I remembered her size from my shopping excursion on Martha's Vineyard, and I'd bought both as a surprise for her. Never did I think I'd give them to her under these circumstances. My mind refused to stop visualizing how she was attacked and each version was worse than the previous one.

I should've known she was a survivor of abuse and looking back, the signs were there. I was furious with myself that I didn't recognize what was happening to her.

I could've gotten her out earlier.

I could've defended her.

I walked around the kitchen in *Cerberus'* lower deck, gathering some ingredients to make her a decent sandwich, hoping I could convince her to eat. I had no clue what I was doing, though.

I listened to the water running in the shower and it only seemed to amplify all the thoughts funneling through my head.

Ana hadn't been in shock over her father's violence. She seemed to accept it. Make sense of it. For her not to be shaken by the past few hours meant one thing: she'd become accustomed to the abuse.

How long had she endured such a nightmare? Months? YEARS?

I heard the water shut off and tried to shake myself out of the emotional rollercoaster I was on. She was looking for me to be the Kian she knew – the one that made her laugh and teased her. She needed that right now, but what I needed was to heal her. I wanted to feel my Fallen marks rise to my skin and flow over her bruises, erasing her pain.

But I couldn't help her while she was awake. I couldn't show her who I truly was, for in the end, how was I any different from her father in terms of violence?

I kill. He hits.

I listened for movement in the bathroom, but didn't hear anything. I stepped closer to the door, and could hear her sniff.

"Ana? Are you okay?" I asked cautiously. She didn't answer and I eased open the door.

What I witnessed nearly broke me.

Ana sat on the tile floor, the towel wrapped around her too thin body, her forehead resting on her arms that crossed over her knees. She didn't look up when I came in, and I ran my eyes over her exposed skin.

The bruises on her face weren't her only ones. Black and blue marks marred her upper arm and back, like a child's enthusiastic finger painting.

"Aw, Pix. What'd he do to you?" I breathed as I sank down in front of her.

"I was reading," she said without looking up. "It was late and I had the lights on in my bedroom. I didn't hear him come home, but he'd been drinking. Heavily. He saw the light under my door, thought about all the money I was wasting in electricity, and he snapped. I wasn't ready for it and got cornered in my room." She sighed, "I'm normally a lot better at not getting cornered."

I could see the goosebumps begin to speckle her exposed skin, so I reached over and grabbed another soft towel, covering her back with it and rubbing her shoulders gently.

She finally looked up at me and her lip trembled as she spoke. "I thought this time would be different, you know? I thought this time he'd think of me first. That I would matter."

Her voice began to crack as a tear rolled down her cheek and disappeared into the towels. "Why won't he change, damn it? Why's it so hard for him to just remember *me* before he reaches for the bottle? I don't understand!"

I leaned forward, resting my forehead against hers. "I'm so sorry. I wish I could fix it – fix him, for you. And I don't think he's going to change, but I'm here. I'm not going anywhere and I swear to you, I'll never hurt you."

She looked at me and I wiped away another tear that had slid free of her eyes. "Thank you for letting me stay," she replied and tipped her face up, pressing a timid kiss to my lips.

It was meant to be simple; to be a casual act of gratitude.

It was anything but.

Ana blinked, startled by what she had done. As if she'd done it without thinking.

I, however, knew exactly what I wanted and what I was doing. I reached up with both hands and carefully cupped her battered face, kissing her back.

I felt her take a sharp breath, her body frozen, but as I cautiously ran my lips over hers, she began to relax. As her body warmed and her breathing turned to deep, heady drags, I felt her hands travel up to rest against my chest.

I broke from the kiss, worried she was about to push me away, but in her eyes I saw the trust I'd been so desperate to earn for weeks.

I felt her fingers tracing the contours of my chest through my t-shirt and I realized she was exploring. She was allowing herself to be in the moment and live, rather than always thinking of how to survive. The light brush of her fingertips was probably going to kill me.

She blushed and smiled at me, and in her face I saw something that looked like affection. Maybe even the beginnings of love. No one had ever looked at me like that – not even Mary. I pushed back the memory of what I had done to her, refusing to let the past destroy our moment.

I stroked Ana's undamaged cheek. "I'm making you some lunch. How about you get dressed and come eat?"

She raised a curious eyebrow. "Since when do you cook?"

"Umm . . . since now?"

Ana looked dubious. "Tell you what – how about we both avoid food poisoning and I cook? You'll be impressed by my culinary abilities!"

Hiding what I really was from Pix was going to require some fancy maneuvering on my part – especially the food thing. "I, uh, actually don't eat often. I have a weird genetic metabolism thing. I already ate for the day, but I'm happy to keep you company."

"You eat ONCE A DAY?" she asked, floored.

Technically I didn't eat food at all, but I could probably get away with the once-a-day fairy tale.

I stood, offering her a hand so she could get up off the tile. "Yes, because some of us are just that amazing."

She laughed as I pulled her to her feet, offering a snide remark about my weird eating habits, and suddenly I had my Pixie back.

The one who made my world better, who challenged ME to be better, and who I was determined to never fail.

30

 ANA

I KISSED HIM, AND DOING so pushed away the sharp memory of my father's hand and the unyielding edge of my bureau. The way Key's hands drifted over my face, so gentle, were a heady contrast to the urgency I felt in his rock hard body.

It was as if he was pulling himself back, slowing himself down. As if he wanted to make sure I felt . . . safe.

Feeling safe was not something I ever dwelled on before. I just assumed life was a constant fight to stay above the undertow that was trying to ruin me.

But with Kian, life bloomed in Technicolor. I saw the world differently, realized that those things that had always been dragging me down, couldn't reach me when I was with him.

It was only now that I understood WHY I felt so different with him. It was because I felt safe. Accepted.

Adored.

I finished changing into the clothes he'd bought for me at the Boarding House, amazed he had been thoughtful enough to buy me a gift when I'd given him nothing.

The second bedroom he'd offered me to stay in was beautiful, with a large oval bed and dark wood furniture. The mass of pillows and blankets spread over the bed looked as though they tumbled out of a design catalog, daring me to flop into them.

I would've too, but I was hungry and not exactly convinced Kian, the non-eater, could cook.

I finally made my way out of the bedroom and down the hallway to where Kian was waiting in the galley. He gestured to the glass and chrome kitchen around him. "Mi casa es su casa."

"Pfft – tu no tenga una casa. Tenga un barco grande," I rattled off in dusty Spanish, certain he only knew that one phrase he offered.

Uh, I was wrong.

He began talking in rapid fire Spanish and I had no clue what he was saying, though he had an irritatingly sure smile spread on his face as he yammered.

I raised my hand, stopping him mid monologue. "Okay, okay! I yield. English, por favor."

"I may lose to you in many ways, Pix, but Spanish? I've got that one down. Now, what do you want for lunch? Sandwich?" he asked, gesturing to the weird assortment of food he had pulled out.

"Hmmm," I mused, not convinced I could make something edible out of Kian's choices.

I wandered over to the fridge and began looking inside. For a dude that barely ate, he sure had a great selection of food. I reached for a pear when I suddenly heard the parlor door above us slide open and MJ's voice echo through the yacht. "Kian! Are you here? Is Ana with you?"

"Yeah, MJ! We're down below!" Kian called back. He then leaned down quickly and gave me a peck on the lips, stalling my heart.

"What was that for?' I whispered as I heard MJ descending the stairs.

"Because I bet my cow print trunks that Apron Boy is going to end up hanging with us and acting like a chaperone for as long as possible. I figured I better get in one more taste of your lips before he got down here, especially since all I want to do is kiss you. Constantly."

I was staring at Kian, wide eyed as MJ finally rounded the landing into the kitchen. "Hey – I just wanted to make sure you weren't headed home. Are you okay?"

I didn't respond, still running the whole *kiss you constantly* thing through my mind. Could people actually do that? Wouldn't they eventually need to breathe? Or pee?

"Hello? Ana?" questioned MJ again, finally catching my attention.

"What?" I asked, peeling my gaze away from Kian.

MJ was glancing between the two of us. "I asked if you were okay. I don't want you going back home. I thought

181

we could camp out on Sandy Neck. I've got my tent and sleeping bags and – "

"I, uh, I'm actually staying here. On the boat."

"With me," added Kian.

MJ laughed. "Oh yeah right. Like THAT's a good idea! Half the time you two are arguing, and the other half . . . No. NO. You two together? Here? HELL NO."

I crossed my arms, defiant. "Oh for crying out loud, it's not that big of a deal. Plus, Kian has a spare room. We're just . . . friends." *With epic benefits!*

MJ looked at Kian, then back to me. He sighed. "It's like trying to convince the out-of-state drivers that they can go around the rotary more than once. I give up, but Kian – you better not be toying with Ana. Or me. She has enough shit in her life without adding another jerk who will just use her and lose her."

"HEY! I'm standing right HERE!" I snapped.

Kian looked at MJ, all amusement falling from his face. "MJ, I'd never do anything to hurt Ana, and that includes breaking her heart. I swear to you, I want nothing but to make her life better."

"HELLO! I'm STILL HERE! I don't need to be bartered between the two of you! I can make my own damn decisions and if I want to stay here with Kian, or snuggle up against the porta potty at Kalmus beach, it's my decision."

Kian's face contorted. "You'd snuggle up next to a porta-potty? Ew."

I rolled my eyes and flung the pear at him, which he caught easily. MJ however, wasn't amused.

I stepped to him and wrapped my arms around my lean, shaggy-haired friend. MJ was as tall as Kian, but not as broad, and I often had trouble comprehending his shifter ability when he was so slim and wiry as a human.

"I always take everything you tell me to heart, MJ, but this time you need to trust me. I promised Kian I wouldn't go home anymore when my dad was around. I swear to you, I'm not going to try to fix him anymore. You were right. You were always right – Dad needs to fix himself and I can no longer be the target of his anger."

MJ gave me a squeeze and I winced, the bruise on my arm and back tender. "Careful, MJ. I'm kinda sore."

He quickly let me go, looking me over with a worried expression. "It's more than your face?"

I shrugged. "It'll heal."

He looked at Kian who simply answered where all the bruises extended. I thought MJ was going to punch a wall.

"Can we, you know, change gears? Please? I was just about to make lunch. How about you join us, MJ?" I asked, moving back to the fridge.

My pal managed a small smile and pointed me towards the table. "I'll cook. You sit. And Kian . . . I don't know. Do something useful."

"See, ordering me around is not the best way to become my wingman. Someday you and I will be friends, MJ. You'll see," said Kian, pulling some ice from the freezer. He began wrapping it in a towel for my face, while MJ listed all the reasons that he and Kian would never be buddies.

As MJ cooked, Kian sat next to me, holding the towel to my face, and the way he looked at me left no doubt: Kian O'Reilly wanted a better life for me, and felt my pain equally.

31

I DIDN'T GET ANA AND MJ'S choice of movies at all. I mean, some of the motivations behind these characters made no sense. Even weirder, why did the kid everyone called "Chunk" even tolerate the name? And what in the hell was a truffle shuffle? I saw no truffles and he was just standing there, jiggling like a stack of pasty Jell-O.

"This is why I don't watch movies. Hollywood makes zero sense to me," I replied as I leaned back on the couch in *Cerberus'* parlor. Ana was snuggled into a blanket on the other end of the couch while MJ laid on the floor, all three of us watching the flat screen attached to the far wall.

After lunch, the darkening sky quickly turned to rain, thus limiting us to few activities. Movies seemed to be the best option, especially since MJ had stacked about ninety in the back of his Wrangler along with his camping gear. We could've gone to the actual theaters, but Ana's face was pretty bad and I didn't want people staring at her. I didn't think she wanted the attention either, especially if she saw a classmate.

It was one thing to be in the spotlight for the positive things in life, but she didn't need the world to know that someone knocked her around.

God help us if we ran into that bitchy, prima donna Nikki – she nearly blew a screw when we were demolishing her volleyball team during Teddy's party. She had muttered some choice words about Ana and MJ, and while they hadn't heard her, I caught every word clearly. She was brutal and didn't miss much, including her assessment of Ana's MIA mother and MJ's family's tiny shop.

I tried hard not to dwell on Nikki's venomous words, nor the fact that Pix's abuser was her father, especially since I couldn't retaliate and murder either of them. My level of self-control was bordering on pure torture . . .

"Okay, you're obviously not seeing the brilliance that is Goonies," replied MJ. "You take this crazy cast of rejects that do NOT fit well together, throw in a treasure hunt and bad guys, and voila! Best friggin' movie EVER!"

Ana smiled at me and she munched happily on a handful of M&Ms. "Seriously. You need an education on Spielberg. I say we do a marathon of only his films."

"AMEN to that!" hooted MJ.

I moaned. "Is all his stuff about kids chasing pirate treasure? I need something, I don't know, scary I guess." Heck, it better be downright chilling to compete with my everyday life . . . well, up until recently that is. The last person I had killed was Benton, though the animal kingdom probably had me listed on a Most Wanted poster at this point.

While I hadn't thought of Sam Benton in a while, I found it suspicious that there had been no mention of his "overdose" in any news outlets. And, granted the press didn't cover every overdose or suicide, but I'd left him in a 1935 Auburn – I'd dare say that was probably a first, even by drama-addicted news stations' standards.

About a week after I'd killed him, I paid his house a visit, slipping inside in the dead of night – an ability made easy since he was WAY past dead. No homeowner equalled no need for permission to enter. I was curious if his body was still where I left it, since there was no mention of his death in any of the papers. But his body, and car, were gone. No police tape, no finger printing dust . . . nothing.

To me, the lack of any sign of police presence meant one of two things: that the cops really bought the overdose thing and it was an open and shut case of drug dealer killed by his own product, or the people Benton worked for came looking for him and his ride, and found both before the cops did.

Quite frankly I was hoping for the second scenario, since I'd never have to worry about Pix finding out that the car she fixed was related to a murder . . . and thus, to me.

"KIAN! Pay attention! Dinosaurs or sharks?" asked Ana, poking me in the leg with her foot. I wanted to grab her and tickle her and then silence her squeals by pressing my lips to hers.

I managed to control that urge.

"What?" I asked, totally confused as I had entirely zoned, my mind dwelling on Benton.

"Do you want to see a movie about killer dinos or a killer shark?" she asked, acting as though I'd be scared out of my wits with either choice.

"Shark, of course," I replied.

32

 ANA

MJ LEFT BY TEN, HIS MOTHER having called him and demanded he get his butt home since he had to make ice cream at the crack of dawn. He left, reluctantly.

I think he was sure I wouldn't be able to control myself around Kian. Or that Kian would jump my bones in my sleep. It actually rubbed me the wrong way, how he was so sure Kian was hiding crap and that I was a hormone-driven idiot.

I wasn't a moron and Kian had been nothing but good to me, though the two of them were still icy to one another. I started to fret that MJ was getting jealous of having to share me with Kian. I suspected he was worried that Kian and I were destined for something more than friendship and that he'd be left as a third wheel, which was crazy.

MJ was my family. No guy would ever replace that . . . even if he could make a single kiss melt my mind.

And Kian's kiss? Damn near superhuman.

I watched him from my spot at the kitchen counter, my steaming cup of hot chocolate nestled between my palms. He had changed into a pair of blue sweatpants and a black t-shirt and sat at the table, charting a map of the South Shore area with a steel ruler and pen. His deep, smooth voice seemed to fill the galley area like a rich smoke.

"I'm thinking we could head south, maybe hit Newport, Block Island, and Mystic. It's the perfect time of year to head down there and each place has some great festivals going on." He looked up from his map, giving me a soft smile. "Let me steal you away for a while."

I looked down at my mug, rubbing away the chocolate sticking to the lip with my thumb. He thought that I could escape my problems by running away. Truth be told, I *wanted* to take him up on it, but running away never solved anything.

Only the weak fled, and I was determined to stand my ground – to regain the freedom and happiness that had been slowly whittled away from me. I slid out off the barstool and walked over to Key. His beautiful face looked hopeful.

"I can't leave. I have obligations and this is my life. I do *want* a better life, but it has nothing to do with all this," I replied, waving my hand at the yacht's opulence. "I want a solid, happy, hard working life right here, in my hometown."

His smile slid a little. "Am I included in that vision for a better life?" he asked, a little unsure.

I twisted a piece of my hair through my fingers. The purple and black had begun to fade thanks to all the surfing

I'd done with him over the past few weeks, and my deep brown color was starting to show through. In some ways, the dye in my hair had been my act of defiance and determination. It was an armor that made me feel like I had some control in my existence.

But Kian had a strengthening effect on me. All those weird, little pieces of protection that I'd clung to so fiercely were slowly falling away. He took the place of all those things I'd used to guard my back and harden my resolve. He made me stronger, and I felt like the real Ana Lane was starting to peek through as well.

I lifted the pen from his hand and set it on the table. "Yes. I'd like you to be part of that. Of . . . me."

He stood up, forcing me to step back. "And how do you see me, in this vision of your future? Am I a friend?"

"Yeah," I whispered. My stupid heart was vibrating, causing my voice to turn breathless. This wasn't me – I wasn't the girl who swooned for hot guys, but with Kian, it was so different. He was so different.

"Can I be more than a friend?" he asked quietly.

I simply nodded and he slowly reached out, easing my hair from my fingertips and smoothing it over my sore back. He drew his fingers softly down my neck and shoulder, as if trying to brush the bruises from my skin.

As he touched me, he seemed hurt and angry all in the same moment. "Why? Why would he ever do this to you? He has no right . . ."

I put my hand to his lips, stopping him from talking. "He blames me, but he also loves me in his own way. His hands weren't always used for hitting."

Kian gently pulled my fingers from his mouth. "What you think of as love, is not love. I would never hurt you like this," he pledged, running his hand over my purple cheek. "I may make mistakes and I may not always say the right thing, but I swear to you, you are safe with me. No matter what, remember that I'm a safe place for you and I want you to find your dreams. I want to help you find your flawless life."

Something inside me cracked. A piece of that armor I always wore gave way, and for the first time in years, I believed in a better future. I saw myself happy and free. I must've started crying, because Kian wiped something wet from my cheeks and whispered that it was going to be okay.

He began kissing away my tears and all I wanted was to stay with him forever. To bring him along as we chased our dreams and blazed our own destinies.

I was falling brutally hard for him and I could no longer hide it. I no longer wanted to.

I turned my mouth to his and suddenly we were kissing. It was soft and stunning and made my head spin. His hands slipped to my hips and my fingers took on a mind of their own, traveling to the back of his neck and over his chest.

Soon the kiss became stronger, hungrier, and Kian's hands were sliding to the front of my belly, slipping under the hem of my shirt. His fingers stopped at my belly button ring and I felt his lips smile against my own.

I broke the kiss. "Are you grinning?" I asked, the pain of a few moments before lifting with his fabulous smile and warm palms.

I'd remained numb for years – closed off to the world as a form of survival. But with Kian, I felt everything, and what I felt in his arms was intense beyond words. And though I was certain that getting romantically tangled with Kian was akin to playing footsie with the devil, I wanted it. I believed I could handle it, like daring myself to walk across the scorching blacktop, barefoot.

"I'm admiring your jewelry," he replied, a wicked grin on his lips. "You really are such a girlie girl."

"WHAT? I'm NOT a girlie girl!" I snorted.

"You have belly button bling. Naval jewels are girlie girl things. Tattoos . . . those are the stamp of the hardcore chicks. I bet you even have pink underwear with rhinestones."

I narrowed my eyes, slowly catching on to his devious plotting. "Wait a minute, you sneaky brat, are you trying to get a look at my undies?"

He wasn't the least bit ashamed. "Maybe. Any chance it's working?"

"NO," I laughed, though my insides were doing circus stunts. "Plus, I don't have pink underwear. THAT goes to show you how little you really know me." What a lie – he truly *saw* me, possibly more than MJ. He didn't see me as broken, despite how bad I looked.

He saw me, the real Ana, and he was totally teasing me. Baiting me. He did it because he knew it was what I needed.

"You're right. Bad me. I shouldn't be asking such things," he replied, dropping his lips dangerously close to mine, his blue eyes never breaking contact with me. My belly ring turned easily in his fingers, which was driving me insane in the most delicious ways. He was seducing me . . . or trying to.

Two could play at this game.

I rolled my body towards him, pinning his wandering hand between us and brushing my lips along his . . . then pretended to yawn. "Oh, man, I'm beat. I'm going to head to bed. I'll see you in the morning."

I stepped away from him suddenly and started to head to my room, leaving Kian standing there with a devilish grin on his face.

"Hey – is it always this hot in here?" I asked, looking back at him innocently and fanning my t-shirt. "I hope you don't mind, but I think I'm just gonna sleep in my underwear tonight," I said, reaching the door.

He was still watching me silently, almost like a wolf studies its prey. The effect made heat race through my chest, but I was undaunted.

"I hope your sheets have a high thread count, since, you know – my belly bling can get caught on the cheaper sheets. I tend to move around a lot in my sleep. Like, A LOT."

Kian's face slipped into scowl. "You're not playing fair."

I stepped into my room, just my face appearing in the door as I smiled back at him. "Oh, and sometimes I'm loud, too. You know, talking and whispering. Heck, even moaning in my sleep. I hope I don't keep you up, you know, worrying about my belly button ring and all the moaning. But anyway — goodnight!"

With that I shut my door and tried not to laugh as I heard Kian demand if I was trying to torture him.

33

 ANA

I COULDN'T SLEEP. By three in the morning, I was desperate for some shut eye, but there was no lock on the bedroom door.

I needed a lock on the door.

I needed a bureau that could slide in front of it.

I needed the round bed to be square and wedged in the corner, so the wall could guard my back.

It was ridiculous. My father wasn't on the yacht, nor would he look for me here. He probably wouldn't look for me at all.

They say that prisoners of war have trouble letting go of their survival techniques, even when they are rescued. As I stared at the door, trying desperately to convince myself that I was safe, I understood the hell they lived in, even once they were home. They clung to those things and behaviors that kept them alive, because some horrors become the monsters in the night that stalk you.

My memories were stalking me something fierce, and my body was screaming for sleep.

I finally sucked up my courage and got up, dragging the heavy comforter from the bed along with a pillow.

Quietly, I left my room and moved down the darkened hallway towards Kian's, following the little blue lights embedded in the polished floor. I eased open his door, allowing my vision to adjust to the room's blackness. Sleeping on the bed was Kian, one sculpted arm tossed over his face, his perfectly cut torso rising and falling with steady breaths.

I slipped around his bed to the far side of the room, placing the blanket and pillow on the floor near the wall, and easing my aching body down onto the ground. Framed by the wall on one side of me, and Kian's bed on the other, I could now keep the monsters at bay.

This felt safer. Like no rage could reach me here because I was protected on all sides, like a child stacking stuffed animals around them, a defense against the Boogie Man.

I stiffened, though, when I heard the bed move, the sound of fabric sliding against fabric. I could hear Kian stepping onto the floor, but then I felt him lay down next to me, his body warming mine as I kept my back to him. I was acutely aware of every place we connected.

I felt like a kid getting caught doing something wrong, so I tried to explain. "You don't have a lock on the bedroom doors."

"No, but I'll install one tomorrow if you'd like," he replied, his voice softened by the velvet darkness. He carefully placed one strong arm around me and I realized I was shivering. Somehow the strength of his arm soothed my trembling, but also unlocked the brutal memories stored in my nightmares.

"I had one at home. I'm used to having one." My voice sounded dry – half dead.

"Okay."

"I can't sleep without it," I whispered, and Kian held me tighter, his breath tripping over my skin.

"God, I'm so sorry, Pix. I should've known. Should've gotten you out and protected you sooner."

I reached up to his arm that crossed my chest and ran my hands along its strong contours as I shifted my body to look at him. In the blackness, the cut of his face seemed almost too flawless.

"It's not your fault, Key. You had no clue."

He started to protest, but I touched his lips with my fingers. "Not your fault."

He turned his face into my hand, as if I could comfort him. "Whatever you need, Pix, just ask. Are you okay here with me? I can sleep on the floor, but you should take the bed. This can't be comfortable for you, with . . ." his voice trailed off.

"With the bruises. You can say it. And if it's okay with you, I'd rather stay here, near the wall and you." I yawned, my fingers grazing the wall and my back tucked against Kian's chest.

"It's fine with me, Pix. Get some sleep," he whispered, tucking his face against my neck.

With Kian guarding my back, I quickly fell into a dreamless sleep.

34

⤳ KIAN ⤳

ANA WAS A COMBINATION OF thrilled and stunned the next morning as she looked in the mirror. All her bruises had faded to almost nothing, and she couldn't figure out why . . . not that she was complaining.

I was sure she wouldn't be so thrilled to know that I had healed her in her sleep, thanks to a few stolen deer souls.

I probably shouldn't have done it, but I couldn't handle the sight of what that bastard had done to her. I couldn't let her suffer when I had the ability to repair her fair skin and sore muscles. I could take away her physical pain, but sadly not the memories of how she got them.

MJ had swung over to the yacht early in the morning, bringing with him breakfast consisting of blueberry muffins and fresh ground Nirvana coffee. He took one look at Ana and his gaze slid to me. His focused appraisal made me uneasy.

My kind was a rare, urban legend to this area – a campfire story told by parents and designed to scare kids into submission. But like all legends, there was truth behind the lies.

I was the reality behind the grim fairy tale.

MJ Williams never did like me much, but the way he looked at me while peeling chunks of pastry from his breakfast, was unnerving – like an enemy, sizing up his foe.

"I drove by your house this morning," he finally said to Ana as she sat cross-legged on the sofa, braiding her hair. "Your dad's truck was gone and *Charlotte* is not at the dock. The harbormaster said they were headed to Georges Bank. He said your dad mentioned pulling a double haul – he's probably going to be gone for two weeks."

Ana tossed her braid over her shoulder and stood. Her eyes lost their shine with the mention of her father. "Well . . . that's good, I guess. I'll head home after work. Thanks for letting me crash here last night, Kian."

I looked at her and all I could think of was how lonely the yacht would seem without her. "I got Jack to give you three days off, Ana. You don't have work today," I replied.

"Seriously?" she asked.

I shrugged. "I just thought you needed a break."

MJ, who'd been watching us intently, offered a suggestion. "How about we all go surfing? Tonight. Cahoon's Hollow. I bet it will be pretty empty due to the surf show in Rhode Island."

Ana brightened. "Sounds awesome! I'm in, but I do need to swing home and change. And I can pack us a picnic dinner – sound good?"

"Sounds good. What about you, Kian? You in?" he asked, causing a weird sense of unease to climb up my spine. His friendly invitation felt more like a set-up.

"Sure. I'm in," I replied, carefully. "Can I have a moment with Ana, though? Alone?"

MJ gathered his stuff. "Of course. I'll see you guys later. Ana – want me to pick you up at your place? Say, sixish? I have the afternoon off from the shop."

"Sounds good to me," she chirped, giving him a hug. "Thanks for breakfast."

"Sure. I'll see you later," he replied, then headed out of the parlor and down the dock.

I turned to Ana. "You don't have to be alone in your house. You can stay here. I'd like you to stay here."

She looked around the yacht, playing with her fingertips. "I'm sorry about last night. I didn't mean to wake you up."

I reached out to her side and she looked at me, shame in her eyes. "If you need me to sit outside your door and sing nursery rhymes until dawn, I will. I'll share my bed with you, I'll push it against the wall so you feel boxed in, where no one can get you, ever."

I took her face in my hands, lowering my own to within inches of her lips. "Stay with me, Pix. Let this place be your home as well. Nothing will ever harm you here, trust me."

She looked at me with those incredible eyes, and a smile lifted to her face. "You're a bad influence, you know that? You'll end up corrupting my morals."

I smiled at her, loving her sass. "Wait — you have morals? Because I could've sworn you were talking about underwear and moaning not long ago."

"I didn't say they were good morals, did I?" she whispered as she leaned up to kiss me, her soft lips messing with my mind.

Kissing Ana was better than any high I'd ever gotten from stealing a soul, but the knowledge that she'd been living in hell, burned through my heart like acid.

35

MJ WAS RIGHT — CAHOON'S WAS deserted, just as he had predicted. With the Ripster Surf Show going on in Rhode Island, the beach was ours alone, which was a damn good thing since he was currently stripping behind the bathhouse.

Though he'd gotten really good at shifting into his dog form, he quickly learned that doing so while still fully clothed, resulted in nearly being strangled by his American Eagle duds. He still hadn't forgiven me for cutting him out of his signed Led Zepplin t-shirt, but his doggy lips were literally turning blue from being throttled around the neck.

I finally heard a sharp bark and turned around to see Marsh in his hairy dog form trotting up to me. To the rest of the world, MJ now appeared to be a huge, black canine . . . and the most obedient, smart one on the face of the earth.

Marsh made Lassie look like a total idiot.

MJ was convinced that all nice guys liked dogs – that they would show kindness and affection to animals, especially a canine that belong to a girl they liked. And while he and Kian seemed to at least be tolerating each other, MJ got really weird after I told him that I was going to stay on *Cerberus*.

Thus, he demanded the "doggie-detector" test for Kian, which seemed pointless to me. Kian would be fine with me having a dog. Well, not REALLY having a dog, but hanging out with a dog . . .

MJ needed more hobbies or a girlfriend, I swear.

When he pitched his plan to me a few hours ago, I argued he was psychotic, but I finally agreed to having him become Marsh for the evening just to get him to stop nagging me. I'd tell Kian that MJ had been delayed at the ice cream shop, and so I brought along his Jeep . . . and the town stray.

Oh my god, this was stupid.

Honestly, I was a little uneasy about Marsh watching over Kian and I while we went surfing, especially since we thoroughly enjoyed kissing. While I hadn't told MJ about my changing "status" with Kian, I suspected he had picked up on something going on between us this morning.

Something I didn't understand completely either.

MJ and I would never be more than best friends, but I felt as though he was slowly getting left out of my normally dull life, which was my fault. As I sat down on the beach next to his warm, hairy body, I silently vowed to spend more time with him and not let Kian come between us. Bros before hos, as they say, and MJ was decidedly a *bro*.

As we sat there, surrounded by the sound of the waves tumbling to shore, visions of my dad's past attempts to get sober forced their way into my head. Visions of the other night, and how pure his rage was invaded my mind.

I tried to distract myself by playing with Marsh's triangular ears, which was a habit that usually made him crazy. I methodically pinned each fuzzy ear down to the sides of his head, then let them pop back up. Marsh allowed me to do it for longer than normal, no doubt understanding what was going on in my head, but he eventually shook me off.

Soon, I heard the rumble of an engine and looked toward the parking lot, watching as Kian pulled in with his awesome Corvette. Marsh turned to watch as well, but the second Kian stepped out of his car, Marsh FLIPPED OUT. It was as if he'd entirely lost his mind and turned into Cujo.

He bolted from the sand next to me, barking in a blood curdling way that chilled me to the bone, hauling ass right for Kian. I was so confused, but managed to race after him, screaming for him to stop. For Kian to get back in the car before Marsh reached him and tore him limb from limb.

Fear and adrenaline flooded my veins, turning my skin to ice as I tried in vain to catch up to Marsh, my feet digging into the sand, slowing me down. I kept yelling for him to stop and for Kian to get away, but Kian didn't move.

Instead, he stepped forward just as Marsh leapt at him, and slammed him against the hood of his corvette with an echoing *bang*.

I stumbled at the sight of Kian so effortlessly stopping Marsh, but it was Marsh's unmoving form sliding from the hood that had me screaming.

I ran for the car, but Kian grabbed me around the waist, jerking me back. "Ana! Don't! He could be rabid! Are you all right? Did he bite you?" he demanded, pinning me to his chest.

"LET ME GO!" I screamed. "He's my friend! What have you DONE? LET ME GO!"

Kian refused to let me free as I thrashed in his arms, trying not to yell at me over my screams. "Ana – no dog would ever come at me like that. Something's wrong with it. I just did the world a favor!"

I couldn't help it – I spun backward and slapped Kian as hard as I could across the face, the impact scalding my hand. He paused for a moment, unfazed, and looked back at Marsh on the ground. "Fine. I'll let you go, but be careful. I don't think I broke its neck."

He released me and I let out a choked sob as I ran to Marsh and dropped to his side, stroking his head. "NO! Oh please, god, no! MJ – can you hear me? Don't be dead! I swear I'll listen to you! MJ! WAKE UP!"

I turned back to Kian with Marsh's head clutched in my arms and panic swamping my heart. "WHAT HAVE YOU DONE!"

Kian's face looked confused for a moment. "Did you just call that dog . . . *MJ?*"

I could only nod as tears streaked my face. In that moment I didn't care if the world knew my best friend was a shape shifter. I didn't care if the world knew my father could hit me so hard I'd black-out. All I wanted was MJ to be all right.

I'd sacrifice everything to fix him.

Kian swore and walked over to Marsh, kneeling beside him. He looked at me, but his eyes seemed to be a darker shade of blue than I'd ever seen before.

"Ana – I need the truth, right now. Is MJ a Therian? Is your FRIEND a bloody shifter? Christ, did I just knock out MJ?"

I drew a staggered breath. "Yeah, but you can't tell anyone. I trust you not to tell anyone. I don't know why he freaked out. We were just waiting for you."

Kian let out another string of curses. "Shit. I know why he freaked out."

"Why? Why'd he go after you?" I sniffled.

"Because . . . I'm a Mortis. A soul thief," he replied, in a low voice.

No. It wasn't possible. He couldn't be.

My heart hammered in my ears as I stared at Kian. I knew what a Mortis was from Dalca. That crazy gypsy had spoken of her absurd myths and of those who came to Cape Cod to hunt the souls of humans – specifically, swimmers. And yeah, my ability was not normal and MJ's was, well, damn near alien. But I never believed her twisted tales of soul sharks, with their stunning beauty, immortal lives, and inhuman strength and speed.

She said they were killers, perfectly skilled in the art of making murder look like an accident. She also said that MJ would know one if he came across one while in a phased form. That he would be able to sense their soulessness, like the scent of a poisonous flower.

She also said that a Mortis had the ability to heal someone. Holy crap, last night I was covered in awful shades of purple and black, but this morning my skin was nearly perfect.

Kian must've *healed me* in my sleep. He tossed MJ because he was protecting himself and me.

I shoved down my fear and went on faith and hope that Kian was not a threat to me. "Fix him. I know you can heal an injury. Fix him. *Please.*"

Kian narrowed his gaze at me and suddenly I truly saw him, a lethal version of Gatsby, with his perfect life full of lies set inside a gilded world of privilege. To anyone else, that was all he was – a handsome man with a flawless life.

They didn't see the killer.

They also didn't see the man that I did.

"You're not afraid of me, are you?" he asked, amazed.

I grabbed him by the shirt. "Listen up, Shark Boy! Are you gonna help him, OR NOT?" I demanded.

Kian looked a bit floored.

36

WHILE MY KIND DIDN'T DREAM, something was wrong because, sure as shit, I was enduring one twisted hallucination: Ana Lane seemed to know the details about my kind. Even more shocking was the fact that she wasn't running to the next state, screaming for torches and pitchforks.

MJ being a Therian was definitely a mind bender, but I'd run into shifters like him before. Not many, but they were out there . . . including the shaggy black one I just knocked senseless. He was going to be some type of pissed when he woke up.

Ana was glaring at me, half angry, half terrified for her friend.

"I . . . well, yes. I can heal him, except that I didn't really injure him. I just knocked him out."

"YOU CALL THAT A NON-INJURY?" she demanded at the top of her lungs.

Ana was nothing if not direct. I'd bet the yacht that if an alien ship landed in a handicap spot, right then and there, she'd tell them to move.

I reached down and felt the dog's pulse just to make sure I didn't accidentally do more damage than I thought. It beat strong and steady under my fingers. "He'll eventually wake up."

Ana smacked me in the arm. "And when exactly is 'eventually' because not ALL of us are friggin' immortal. Supposedly."

How was she not freaking out about all of this? Pix was so far from sane – no wonder I liked her. "It depends on him, really. He could wake up in an hour or in a matter of – "

MJ bolted up so fast that he knocked Ana onto the pavement. He then took one look at me and flipped the switch to psycho dog once again. He launched at me, but in my crouched position, with my attention on Ana, I didn't move fast enough and MJ slammed into me.

Damn, the kid was strong in his dog form.

He pinned me to the pavement and I wrangled his head into my hands, trying to keep his teeth from reorganizing my face. "LISTEN to me, you dumb ass! I'm not a threat to you! I don't hunt humans!" I yelled, though that last bit was debatable.

I gave him a hard shove, but MJ was fast, clamping down on my arm in a vicious bite, which hurt like hell. I swore, trying to pry him off me without snapping his jaw, but then Ana was there, pushing MJ back. He finally released and Pix flung herself over me, acting as a human shield.

I didn't want her getting between the furry moron and me, so I tried to push her off but she snapped her head to look at me, and I froze. In her eyes there was a clear demand for me to stand down.

She turned her attention back to MJ, whose hackles were raised and his head was low, my blood smeared on his mouth. He was growling, his ears pinned back, but he wasn't coming at me anymore.

Not with Ana in the way.

"MJ, stop. Please stop! He's not a threat to me. To us," she looked over her shoulder at me once again and something in her eyes – an unspoken faith and hope that she wasn't making a huge mistake – made my heart seize. "I trust him," she whispered.

MJ, still growling, glared at me, then looked to Ana. She reached out to stroke his head, but he moved from her touch, causing Ana to sigh sadly. "You, above all people, know that I've been happier this past month than I've been in years. I owe so much to you. You hold my secrets and I trust you always. But please don't do this to me – don't tear me between you and Kian."

She looked at me once again, though she was still addressing MJ, and I swallowed hard.

"Kian may be one of them – one of the soul sharks Dalca warned us about. And yes, he may be a monster, but he's also a man, and over the last month he's never shown me his dark side."

She drew a quaking breath and added quietly, "When I'm with him, I feel free."

In that moment, all I saw was Ana, with her black hair, sea storm eyes, and unmarred skin. In that moment I was not a monster at all, but a man falling hard for the one girl I shouldn't.

"I'm more human than I've ever been in my life when I'm with you," I said to her, then looked to MJ. "I can't change what I am, but I can choose to live a life within the confines of my fate. I swear, MJ, she's safe with me."

Ana was still studying me, and finally turned back to MJ, who had stopped his incessant growling.

His huge brown eyes looked over the two of us – Ana in my lap and my arm bleeding. He finally slouched into a sitting position and let out a disgusted snort, finally giving in.

Ana let out a sigh of relief and gestured to MJ. "Kian, meet Marsh, also known as the town stray. I obviously can't call him *MJ* when he's in his dog form, so he's Marsh when he's like this."

I nodded. "Right. Marsh." I looked at the huge dog who was still glaring at me. "So, uh, how 'bout a truce?"

MJ – I mean *Marsh* – snarled.

Terrific.

37

⮜ KIAN ⮞

A HALF HOUR LATER, I sat on my couch facing Pix. She had insisted on checking out the wound on my arm even though I'd explained, repeatedly, that it would heal quickly.

She eased my shirt off and began cleaning the set of holes in my arm carefully, shooting MJ a look of death every once in a while. Apron Boy, who'd phased back into his irritating self at the beach, was leaning against *Cerberus'* bar area.

Ironically, he also looked like he wanted to kill someone – mainly, me.

I cleared my throat and Pix looked up at me. "You really don't have to fuss over me," I protested, but Ana just shushed me, focused on the task at hand like a defiant version of Florence Nightingale.

"Yeah, Ana – you DON'T HAVE TO fuss over the soul sucker," snapped MJ.

I pointed at his head. "Watch it, fur ball. If I recall, I didn't go after you like some cracked-out sociopath. I was just there to surf with you guys, but NO. You had to go and make me smell like wet dog and add a few gouges to my arm. You owe me an apology."

MJ laughed hysterically. "Hell NO! You come here, acting like you're some saint, lied to Ana to get in her pants, and you expect us to OVERLOOK that fact that you're a killer? You're delusional."

"HEY!" snapped Ana. "Where do you get off, thinking that you know better than me? I can handle myself and Kian sure as hell hasn't been anywhere near my pants!"

Sadly, this was true.

She began wrapping gauze around my arm, continuing to lecture MJ on all the reasons none of us were perfect. The girl was fierce when she was on her soapbox. "I can't believe you are making judgments, MJ, especially with our own abilities. Nobody is perfect, and you and I are pretty damn far from normal."

MJ slammed his hand down on the countertop, furious. "He's a KILLER! Turn your brain on and your hormones off!"

"That's ENOUGH!" I yelled, angry he was being such an ass to Ana. "I get it – on the whole 'fucked up' scale of life, I'm majorly skewed towards the negative side. But I've NOT been a threat since I met you two, so stop holding the whole 'killer' part over my head!"

"You say it as if being a murderer is a small part of who you are and barely matters. It's all that matters!" snapped MJ.

"ZIP IT!" demanded Ana, hopping to her feet. "I'm DONE with this stupid bickering! We WILL figure this out, and if Kian says he's only hunting animals, I believe him. I've no reason to doubt him."

"Yet," added MJ.

Ana turned and studied me closely. She nodded. "Yet. I agree. I have *yet* to doubt you, Key. Don't make me question the logic of continuing to be your friend. Ever. Don't break my heart."

I stood and my height forced her to look up.

"I won't break your heart. I swear." I turned back to MJ, who was standing with his arms crossed, fuming. I held out a hand to him, but he refused to shake.

Instead he pushed away from the bar and headed for the parlor door. He stopped next to Pix and glared at her. "I sure hope you know what you're doing, Ana. Because I can't stand by and watch him destroy you."

He then stormed out of the parlor and down the aft deck of *Cerberus*, heading to the parking lot and his Jeep.

Ana watched him go and I could hear her breathing pick up as she tried to control her emotions. "He won't forgive me," she whispered.

"Yes, he will," I said quietly behind her, though the truth was, I had no clue if I just caused an irreparable rift between two best friends. I couldn't do that to Ana, which meant one thing: I needed to befriend the Ice Cream Idiot.

Ana turned to me and in her eyes I saw all the pain of what the past twenty-four hours had brought. I slowly reached out to her and touched her fair cheeks, gently cupping her face.

"I'll fix it. I'll make MJ see that I'm not a threat. I'll make him see that you're safe with me."

"How? He hates your kind," she replied, frustrated.

"Well, if he hates my kind, then I guess I should show him how to fight a soul thief and win. Rushing me like that at the beach? Bonehead move."

"You're going to show him how to kill a Mortis? Why would you do that? He could end up killing a friend of yours!" She blinked, stunned.

"The only friends I've got are you and MJ, and I'd do anything for you."

"Anything?" she asked, as though such a statement couldn't possibly be true.

I leaned down close to her face, our eyes meeting.

"Anything."

38

 ANA

MY SOUL SHARK WAS A MAN OF HIS WORD.

It had been a week since my father had left and MJ tried to chew on Key, but the two boys in my life were slowly finding a shaky middle ground in their relationship.

As promised, Kian had begun training with MJ on a remote portion of Sandy Neck, though at first, MJ refused the help. When he finally caved in from my begging and nagging, he found that training with Kian was actually really useful.

Kian also insisted that I know a few self-defense moves, and he patiently showed me several ways to drop a man in a heartbeat.

It turns out kneeing a dude in the balls usually tops that list, which I knew from the grabby freshman, but a well-placed finger to the eye is also quite helpful.

It was the Mortis, however, that were the ones Kian really worried about, since neither tactic would slow a soul shark. He made sure I understood everything about the

218

hunting tactics of his kind, and how to avoid placing myself in unsafe situations that might attract a soul shark, like him.

A few hours ago, he let MJ and me watch as he took down a deer. He said that we would only trust him if he let us truly see him for what he was . . . and he was breathtaking as a hunter. He wanted me to know how truly lethal his kind was so I'd never put myself in a dangerous situation with a Mortis, including night surfing.

As I sat on his bed in front of him, studying the lines of his face, I reran how fast and effortless the kill was for him. I remembered his speed, so fluid and instant, like a cobra's death strike. I'd been drilling him with questions since I learned that he was a Mortis, and he obliged me, answering each and every small demand.

No matter how dark his details were, my trust in him never waivered.

"Can you do it again?" I asked, reaching out and touching the places on his skin where I had seen beautiful, black twisted lines appear as he took the life force from the deer.

"Do what again?" he asked.

"Make the lines appear?" I asked, fascinated.

He laughed, "You mean my Fallen Marks? You want to see them again?"

I nodded rapidly and chewed on a fingernail, a smile on my face. I watched as Kian exhaled and closed his eyes, and slowly the lines began to form on his face, bleeding and spreading over his skin in elegant swirls of blackness. They traveled down his arms and chest, dipping and tracing each angle of his perfect body.

He finally looked at me, his blue eyes now entirely black, and I swallowed, awed and a bit unnerved. "Can I touch them?" I whispered.

He picked up my hand and placed it on his chest, holding it there. I flushed from the intimate contact. "Watch," he whispered and I gasped as the marks slowly crawled onto my own skin.

I yanked my tingling hand away and the marks disappeared immediately. "What was that?" I asked, shocked as I flexed my fingers.

"It's how I share my healing ability. It's how I fixed your injuries while you were asleep. I can share the life forces I steal, offering them to heal someone. I can heal almost anything," he replied, allowing the beautiful marks to fade from his body and his eyes return to blue.

He reached out to my face. "That night when you came to my bedroom, I couldn't handle knowing you were in pain. All I could think of was what had happened to you; of how he struck you and knocked you down. Healing you was the only way for me to think I could somehow help you."

I scooted closer to him and his hands traveled to my back, holding me in place. "You've helped me more than you could ever know. I'm brave now," I whispered, drawing my hands through his blond hair.

"You were always brave, Pix. I take none of the credit for your fearlessness."

"Yes, I am," I replied as I pressed my lips to his. I felt his hands tighten on my hips as he drew a sharp breath.

"Pix. . ." he warned in a raw tone that sent heat flying through my body.

"Be brave, Frat Boy. I won't hurt you," I replied, a streak of boldness rushing me from the inside, out. I pulled my shirt over my head, displaying my superhero bra, and I heard Kian swear.

I chuckled as I kissed him. "Told ya they weren't pink."

"Jeez, woman – you are trying to kill me! And . . . is that the Wonder Woman symbol?" he asked between kisses. "Because if it is, it totally suits you."

"Cat Woman," I gasped as his kisses traveled from my face, down my neck to my collar bone. "It's Cat Woman. You need to watch . . . more . . . movies."

Holy hell, whatever his lips and hands were doing was AWESOME. My mind became fuzzy, my body damn near on fire.

Somehow I ended up off the bed and pinned against the wall, my legs around Kian's waist, my brain having left for another dimension.

39

KIAN

I COULD FEEL EVERY INCH of her soft, sweet body moving against me and I vowed to stay right here, against the wall, for the rest of my days. I kept one arm behind her back, trying to keep her from being crushed against the bedroom wall, but my control was shredding. I knew I needed to slow down, but she kept moving and breathing my name as I kissed her. Her skin was hot to the touch and flushed, making me nearly lose my mind.

But then she gasped and it sounded identical to another woman I had known.

Mary.

I stopped kissing her, my breath coming fast as I rested my forehead against the wall with Pix pinned against me. "We should stop," I growled, trying to hold onto my sanity.

I could feel the rise and fall of her chest as she caught her breath, and she turned her head, her sweaty cheek resting against mine. "But I want to," she whispered in my ear.

Shit. I desperately wanted to as well, but I didn't trust myself. Mary was proof of that. I forced the words through my lips. "I don't."

I felt her freeze and then she started to shift away from me, attempting to cover her chest. "Oh. Oh, okay."

I held her tighter, refusing to let her think she was anything less than the most beautiful creature in the world.

"No. You don't understand. I want to. God knows, I really, REALLY want to. But there are things I've done in my past that I can never take back. I could lose control with you and hurt you. I could kill you, by accident. I can't even debate that — my mind won't even fathom it. I refuse to chance it with someone I love."

I heard her swallow and I finally looked down at her face, so close to my own. "I love you, Pix. I'm in love with you."

Her mouth fell open slightly as she looked at me and, quite frankly, I was getting a bit panicked. She wasn't answering me. Hell, what if I just scared her, being all serious and whatnot?

She drew a trembling breath. "I . . . I've fallen for you too. I don't know how, and I know it breaks every law of nature, but I have fallen so hard for you," she whispered.

Something warm and wonderful filled every inch of my body — a feeling of total belonging and acceptance in the eyes of the girl I loved.

I smiled and wiped a sweaty strand of hair from her face. "I'm sorry I can't, but I swear I'll make it up to you in . . . other ways. After all, there are bases that can be explored."

Her eyebrow curved in a devious way. "Oh really? Bases could work, as long as you let me down."

"You don't like being plastered to the wall?" I asked, teasing her.

"Well, yes and no. You see, I'm pretty sure there is going to be an indent in my butt from the light switch that I'm basically sitting on at the moment. I get that you're a bit of a pervert, but I'd rather not have the logo of an electric company on my rear."

I frowned, trying hard not to laugh. "But I really like the lighting concept in this yacht."

"Ha, ha. Put me down, Frat Boy," she demanded with a grin, and I obeyed, tossing her on the bed as she squealed.

40

ANA

AFTER NEARLY A MONTH of living on Kian's yacht, I felt like a different person. I mean, I was still me, but a better version of myself.

More importantly, I was starting to come to terms with my father's alcoholism. I started researching it, understanding the psychology behind it, and gradually I was letting go of the guilt.

On some level I'd always blamed myself for my father's problems. I used to tell myself that my existence caused my mother to leave and him to work so hard. I used to tell myself that if I made more money or was more silent, he wouldn't drink.

But the truth was, his drinking was partly his choice, partly a disease. And I couldn't force him to fight for sobriety. He needed to want to get better, all on his own. Knowing I couldn't fix him, was the hardest part for me.

Living with Kian showed me what it was to be loved without strings attached. To have a place that welcomed me like a friend, and where someone adored me . . . even if he was a soul thief.

Key did put a lock on my bedroom door, but I never slept there. Instead I slept with him, every night, and woke up to his strong arms and soft kisses every morning.

In bits and pieces, I had collected my old life from my house and brought it over to the yacht, but I found that much of it was possessed by ghosts of the past, including my rope bracelet that my dad had given me. I had always fiddled with it, as if it were a wishing device that could free my father from his addictions, but it always failed to make him better.

When Kian realized what it was and who gave it to me, he immediately replaced it with a silver Cape Cod bracelet – a simple, silver bangle that locked around my wrist with a little ball. He said it looked like the rings that we had captured while riding the Flying Horses – that it was a reminder of all the good things in life, rather than memories that dragged me down.

Kian also suggested buying me a new wardrobe, new shoes, new everything – even pink underwear, though I was sure that last one was more for his benefit. At first I resisted, not wanting him to pay my way, but then one night he told me that everything that was his, was mine as well. That he wanted me to live with him permanently, if I was willing.

He said that *Cerberus* belonged to both of us and that we balanced one another, like air and fire.

It was a tempting offer and one I needed to think long and hard about. I would be starting junior year at

Barnstable in a matter of weeks and I wasn't sure if I was even legally allowed to live with Kian without my father's permission.

I had talked to Dad a few times on the phone, and he was always half in the bag. Hearing him slur his words as he demanded my return, hurt my heart. I stopped calling however, when he accused me of sleeping around for money. He said I was just like my mother and I could go to hell.

That conversation was so rough, I ended up retching into the toilet between sobs. I was grateful Kian had left to hunt earlier and therefore didn't see me blubbering.

I hated that – hated when I couldn't hold it together and just push down all the anger and pain. I felt weak and stupid when I cried, and I was pretty sure Kian knew it.

MJ knew I'd rather pluck out an eyeball than cry like a girl. He also knew I preferred zombies and car chases over a romance movie any day, which was why I was thrilled when he got us tickets to the drive-in for the re-release of The Fast and The Furious.

I was currently bouncing up and down in the driver's seat of my Trans Am, clapping my hands like a five year old about to open her gifts on Christmas.

"Jeez woman, calm down. I can't be seen with someone who is obviously nuts. Think of my reputation!"

"HA! Your reputation doesn't even exist, MJ, and you know it. Mine doesn't either – that's the perks of being wallflowers!" I laughed, finally calming down as the previews began to roll.

MJ ran his hand along the dashboard of the TA, picking at the silver pin-striping that was chipping away in spots. "I've got to give you credit, Ana. I really didn't think you were going to get this thing running. Mad props, woman. Seriously."

"Thanks MJ! Some days I didn't think I'd get it running either. And it still has loads of bodywork and some fine-tuning, but it'll all get done. I'm determined."

MJ laughed, "And heaven help anyone who gets between Ana Lane and her determination, eh?"

"Pfft – they'd lose a body part or two, that's for sure."

MJ leaned back in the vinyl seat, sighing. "So Kian told me he asked you to move in permanently. He said you wanted to think about it."

I crossed my arms, tweaked that the guys were talking about me behind my back. I mean, I was happy they were starting to get along and all, but chatting about girl issues – MY issues? Um, no.

"I can't believe you guys talk about me. I need to be OFF LIMITS. It's too weird," I demanded.

"I thought you liked living on Kian. I MEAN, on *Cerberus*," said MJ, giving me a knowing look.

I reached over and pinched the bugger hard. "STOP talking about me behind my back!"

"But it's so interesting," he laughed, trying to snatch my hands as I attempted to grab another piece of his flesh. I managed another hard pinch and he screamed for mercy.

"Okay, Okay! UNCLE! I will tell Frat Boy that we can't discuss all your juicy details anymore." He rubbed his side. "Damn woman, I think you left a mark."

"Serves you right, blabbing about me," I replied, a smug smile on my face.

"You know, he's dragging me along to pick out a birthday gift for you tomorrow. I can't believe you're turning seventeen!"

I smiled. "I can't believe it either! I'm curious what he's going to get me . . ."

"I'll steer him towards the frou frou chick stuff that I know you love so much," laughed MJ, and I glared at him. Finally he turned to me. "Okay, well one last question."

I shot him a dangerous look.

"OH COME ON! All I want to know is if you are taking Kian to Waite's party this weekend, or me? Because you've always taken me, but you haven't asked me yet, so . . ."

I winced. MJ had me there. I'd taken him to Waite's summer gala on the Vineyard for the past two years, and it was always really fun. Waite spared no expense and it was open to the islanders at large, so it was a huge event. Big white circus-like tents, live bands, fireworks . . . it was insane. But this year, I asked Kian to be my date, and he gladly accepted.

"Well, I took you the past two years, and I just thought . . . you know, I should invite Kian."

MJ slapped his hand to his chest and hung his head. "You break my heart!" he sobbed, but then snapped his head up with a grin. "Nah – it's totally cool, 'cause I got tickets to MetalFest in Nashua and it's the same night. HA!"

"WHAT? Damn it! I've been dying to go forever! You better bring me home a shirt, darn you!"

MetalFest. The twerp got tickets to the most epic music festival for hard rockers and metal heads. I'd been trying to grab tickets FOREVER.

"Wait – did you get more than one?" I asked.

MJ nodded, but looked a little sheepish. "Well, yeah. I got two – bought them off of Teddy like a week ago. I figured you were going to take Fluffy's captain to the Waite party, so I asked Cara."

"Cara Roberts? But the girl literally can't stop talking. Just listening to her makes me feel like I'm suffocating," I replied, my eyes wide.

"I know. She does talk a lot, BUT the girl knows her metal bands. Plus – she's nice and I've known her since first grade."

I narrowed my eyes, reading MJ's devious shift in emotion. "How convenient that the music will be so loud you won't be able to hear her talking . . . "

"Huh? What's that? I'm sorry, I can't hear ya. I'm trying to watch a movie, here," he replied with a wink.

SIGNED

CAN915

SIGNED

41

I HAD NEVER BOUGHT a birthday gift for a girl, let alone someone as important as Ana. I wanted it to be perfect and a reflection of how much I truly loved her, which was why I was basically panicking.

"Ya know, you kinda left this to the last minute," MJ observed as he ran his hand over the glass that encased the necklaces at the jeweler's little shop. He was totally enjoying the fact that I asked for his help in picking MY GIRL a gift.

MJ knew the truth, which he reminded me of at every opportunity: he knew Ana better than I did.

I stopped in front of one case that also had a selection of rings. One stunning creation sat nestled in black velvet, twisting over itself like the curls of a wave running endlessly around the circumference of the band. Seated in the dead center, and framed by the golden water, was a perfectly cut blue diamond.

It should be Ana's – a jeweled representation of my raven-haired siren – a priceless gem always at home in the fearsome ocean.

In a perfect world, where my kind didn't exist and men didn't beat their beautiful daughters, I'd ask Ana Lane to marry me with that ring. I'd bring her to a secluded spot, where only the wind and the trees would serve as witness, and pledge my undying love to her as I offered her a chip of the ocean and the entirety of my heart.

But life wasn't perfect, and I could never take away her right to children and a life of in-laws and cookies baked for Santa. My kind was a dead end for her – she could never conceive a child with me, never know my family, and at some point, I would look far younger than her as she naturally aged.

I swallowed hard, forcing down the sharp understanding that while I would love her forever, I could not be hers endlessly. For now, however, she was mine and mine alone. "I don't care if it takes all day, I'm getting her the perfect gift for her birthday tonight. You only turn seventeen once," I replied, forcing myself away from the ring.

"Well, unless you're a soul shark," replied MJ smoothly, though not loud enough for the shop owner to hear us. He was totally enjoying my mad scramble to get Ana the perfect gift and had been zero help so far.

Finally I turned to him, swallowing my pride. "I get it, all right? I get that you don't approve of us, but I do love her and I want her to be happy, just like you do. I've never bought a gift for someone before, especially not a girlfriend, and I could really use some guidance here."

I glanced at the clock on the wall, and sighed. "She's only going to be at work for a few more hours and we've been looking all day. I still need to go grab her cake from the Raven, and get back to the yacht to set up for her party."

MJ leaned against one of the counters and looked out the large windows of the shop at the people passing by on the sidewalk, half hidden by umbrellas in a wide variety of colors. It had been raining since late last night, and I easily recalled how Ana slept soundly in my arms, lulled by the sound of the rain humming over *Cerberus'* smooth shell.

"Kian, the three of us aren't exactly a 'party' ya know? I don't think she cares if you decorate or not."

"I'm decorating, damn it."

MJ turned to me, running a finger along the metal edge of the case. "Can I ask you something?"

I gave a non-committal shrug.

"Have you ever seen Ana wear much in regards to jewelry? I mean, besides that Cape Cod bracelet you gave her to replace her dad's."

I looked back at the case. MJ was right. "Well, I'm not getting her tools. I'm sorry, but that is just NOT an acceptable present. And she's not a jewelry girl, so . . ."

I suddenly realized exactly what she'd love and I grabbed MJ by the shoulder, excited. He nearly jumped a mile. "The Boarding House! Damn – I'm such an idiot!"

MJ pulled himself away from my victorious grasp. "Of course you're an idiot. That's not news, dumb ass."

I ignore MJ's jab and offered a quick thanks to the shop owner as we headed out of the store and into the rain. It took a while to weave our way through the crowded street near the harbor, but I was determined to get Ana the surfboard of her dreams.

MJ, resigned to getting the best possible ride for Ana (and a little excited to browse the elaborate selection of the surf shop), started running down the list of possible options as we headed for the Boarding House shop, our jackets slowly getting drenched.

I listened to him talk about the pros and cons of each board, but he was interrupted by his phone ringing.

"Hang on . . ." he said as he answered the cell and we dodged under a store's overhang.

His face slowly turned to that of confusion as he listened. "No. I haven't. I'm sorry," he said to the caller as he hung up.

"What is it?" I asked.

"That was Jack at RC. He said that Ana left for lunch to head to Rick's junk yard and never returned."

Worry clawed at me and I quickly yanked my phone from my pocket, dialing her number. MJ did the same, but both of us got her voice mail.

I jammed my phone back in my pocket, knowing with absolute dread that Ana would never just skip work. MJ seemed to be of the same mind and we both ran towards the harbor, dodging all the shoppers and angry outbursts from people we bumped into. We finally rounded the corner at the end of the street and the harbor came into view.

There, docked in slip 12 and unloading her cargo, was *Miss Charlotte*.

"Do you see the bastard?" I asked MJ, praying he recognized one of the fishermen on the boat as Ana's dad. I'd never met the man, nor did I ever want to for fear I'd rip his throat out.

MJ shook his head. "I don't see him. We need to get over to Rick's and see if she's there. We need to find her. It isn't like her to just up and ditch work."

"I'll kill him. If somehow he's involved and he's hurt her again, I'll kill him," I whispered, the murderer inside me firing to life once again.

"If he's hurt her again, I'll help you," replied MJ.

42

I Almost never left the shop for lunch, but today was different.

Today I was officially seventeen, and Rick at the junk yard was holding a used shifter for the Trans Am for me. True, it was a bit of a splurge, but I figured a girl could spend a couple of bucks on herself when it was her birthday.

Rick, an awesome older man who always kept his eye out for Trans Am parts for me, had left the shifter behind his rambling shack for me to pick up, since he wasn't going to be around. As I had promised, I slid the fifty dollars I owed him under his backdoor after locating the car part tucked into a soaked box near the back stoop. The rain had been near constant and, at this rate, the puddles were going to turn into mini-ponds.

I carried the box back to my car through the rain, mindful of my half hour lunch break and excited about the birthday party Kian and MJ were plotting for later. Technically I wasn't supposed to know about it, but those two sucked at keeping anything a secret.

As I reached my car, I happened to glance up through the filmy rain and froze. Across the street was my father's beat up truck . . . and my dad.

He was standing by the door, six-pack dangling from his fingers, watching me. Even at a distance, I could see the slight shake to his hands as the rain slid down his forearms, a sure sign the liquor in his veins had taken over his common sense.

I couldn't move as I watched him toss the beer onto his torn fabric seat and slammed the door shut, heading for me.

"Lanie girl, where the fuck you been?" he demanded as he finally made it to my side of the street. I fumbled with my package and keys, dropping both as I begun to panic. I quickly dropped down, sliding my hands through the mud, willing my fingers to find the key, which had disappeared into the puddle by my car.

I cursed my own naïve stupidity, angry that I'd lost track of time. For forgetting to keep track of when *Charlotte* was at sea and when she was in her dock.

Mercifully, my thumb slipped across something metal and I grabbed onto the key. I launched to my feet, trying to clear the mud from the piece of silver salvation, but the search had taken too long.

My dad came around the car wrenching my arm to the side in an iron grip just as I tried to run.

Shocked he'd made it to me so quickly, I dropped the damn key again and came face to face with my father, who maintained a crushing grip on my upper arm.

"You been hidin' from me, girl?" he slurred, already plowed by what smelled like whiskey.

"Dad. You need to let me go. You've been drinking – let me drive you home," I replied, my voice shaking, chilled by the rain and fear. I hadn't been faced with his rage since moving in with Kian, and now my father's anger seemed all the more severe to me – as if the immunity I'd built up to his violence had faded.

Parked almost behind Rick's shop, no one could stand as witness to my father's anger. We were basically alone, and he was furious. In that one moment, there was no bureau or lock to save me. No shifting pal or killer boyfriend to defend me.

In that moment, all I had was myself, and I'd be damned if I was going to take anymore of my father's rage. I was worth more than just the backside of his hand, and I finally knew it.

Believed it.

"Ya been whoring yourself out, ain't ya? Been spending all our money on goddamn parts for that piece of shit race car of yours! I'm slaving at sea, day in and day out, and you're here fuckin' about." He yanked me viciously, but I pulled back hard and he stumbled. My fear had bled to fury, suffocating all sense of reason.

"You bastard," I hissed, the rain soaking through my hair as the sky opened up and dumped half of heaven on top of the world. "I work harder and longer that you ever will! You're drunk and selfish and I'm no longer your little girl."

I was not going to tolerate him any more – not when I finally knew what love truly was thanks to Kian.

"Let me go. NOW!" I snarled at him, tears starting to mingle with the icy rain. "I won't tolerate you anymore. I'm your daughter and, for once, you'll treat me with some respect. I deserve that after all you've put me through, damn you! I've fought for you! Stood up for you! But no more. Let me – "

I didn't see the first hit coming, but it felt as though my cheek had exploded inside my face as my father struck me. For a moment, my sight failed, but then all my anger and resentment exploded, and I swung back with everything I had.

I felt my knuckle crack as my fist connected with his nose, and the rain on his face suddenly turned red over his lips, a sure sign I just broke something of his, along with my hand.

I thought the hit would slow him down – give me a chance to run, but I didn't account for the alcohol in his system, blocking his pain.

He felt nothing. No pain. No love. No remorse.

He wrenched my arm hard, throwing me to the ground and I landed on my shoulder, causing it to give a sickening pop. My entire side lit with agony, stealing the air from my lungs, and any fight I had in me, was flattened under a mountain of pain.

My father muttered a few more words, and I watched as he slowly kneeled near me, grabbing me by the jaw. "Ya ever raise a hand to me again, and I'll beat you into oblivion, ya hear? Ya get your ass home, girl. You're my daughter and I won't have you living with some rich prick."

He squeezed my jaw like a vise, and pain shot through to my teeth. "Whadda ya think – that I ain't worth as much as him? A sixteen year old got no business living in sin with some man, got that?"

My father finally released my jaw, staggering away to his truck across the street. He turned back to me, warning me to get back to work so I didn't make my boss think I was some lazy slut.

I laid on the muddy ground near my car, hidden from view and soaked to the bone by the pouring rain, watching him drive away.

With only the sound of the rain as my company, I whispered a prayer for Jack to realize I was missing. For someone to come looking for me.

As a heavy fatigue set in and the pain began to dull, I wondered, distantly, if my father's rage was truly going to kill me. I wondered if making it to eighteen was a fool's dream in pursuit of a man who no longer existed.

I wondered, sadly, if I'd misread my father all along.

He didn't even realize it was my birthday.

43

KIAN

MJ KNEW WHERE RICK'S WAS, thank god. As we drove there, I ran every horrible possibility through my head, and each was worse than the last.

"It's probably not him," said MJ as we rode in his Wrangler. "I mean, what's the chance he would even cross path's with her? Well, except . . ."

"EXCEPT WHAT?" I snapped, willing the Jeep to go faster.

"There's a liquor store across the street that he likes. The owner overlooks the fact that he's obviously a severe alcoholic. A steady customer is a steady customer, I guess."

I rubbed my face roughly, praying that Ana was okay. That maybe she did flake on work. Maybe she thought she'd taken the rest of the day off, since it was her birthday, and maybe Jack forgot.

As MJ turned the corner, a brown pick up truck nearly side-swiped us, and he swore, struggling to maintain control of the Jeep. He quickly looked over his shoulder at the disappearing truck and turned to me, a look of horror on his face. "That was her dad," he said, almost in a whisper.

"Was she in the truck?" I demanded.

MJ just shook his head. "I don't know. I didn't get a good look, but by the way he's driving, he's already had a few."

"Look!" I shouted, spying Ana's beat up car parked behind some wooden shack that was set back from the road.

MJ floored the Jeep and it launched over the flooded potholes, skidding to a stop as I vaulted out the passenger door.

"ANA!" I called as I tore around the car through the rain. I stopped cold when I saw her huddled on ground near the back tire.

She was shaking badly and it seemed to take all her strength for her to look up at me as I dropped to my knees in front of her. She was clutching her arm against her chest and the side of her face was swelling, nearly forcing one eye closed.

I was afraid to touch her, afraid I was going to cause her more pain, but I needed to move her out of the rain. She was probably in shock and her lips were blue from her soaked clothing.

She gave me a weak smile and it nearly tore me in half. "I fought back, Key. This time, I fought back," she managed to say through her chattering lips, but then she stared to gasp, reality sinking in.

"Shh . . . It's okay, love," I tried to soothe as she begun to sob. Her crying became so severe that I was worried she would hyperventilate and I looked back at MJ, feeling helpless.

He stood watching the two of us from a few feet away, and even as soaked as he was, I could tell he was crying.

I eased my arms around her back and under her legs and she cried out as I lifted her from the ground. "I'm sorry, baby. Hang in there and I'll fix that shoulder, okay? Just hang in there."

Ana bit her lip as she buried her frozen face in my neck, trying not to cry out as I walked to the Jeep with her in my arms.

I was going to kill Harold Lane.

The bastard deserved to burn in hell for all eternity. It was taking every shred of control I had to keep my rage from consuming me. But right now, I needed to push everything else aside, for Ana's sake. She needed me to be the man she loved, not a monster bent on revenge.

MJ raced around to the Jeep and forced the front seat forward as I climbed in with Ana in my arms. Every time I moved, she let out the smallest moan, and it tore me to pieces.

MJ grabbed a blanket out of the back of Ana's car, but then stopped by the smashed box on the ground.

"MJ! Let's go!" I called as he picked up the box. He ran back to where I sat with Ana in my arms, and handed me the blanket so I could cover her, trying to keep her body from slipping into shock. He slammed the seat back into place and dropped the crumpled box on the faded leather.

"What's that?" I asked as he started the Jeep.

"Her birthday gift to herself," he replied angrily, his hate a reflection of my own.

I looked down at Pix, who was mumbling something, as if she was caught in a dream, slipping into a semi-conscious state. The sizable swelling on her face made me worry her father had struck her hard enough to cause a concussion.

"Pix, I'm here. MJ is too. Can you open your pretty eyes for me? You need to stay awake" Her long eyelashes drifted open and MJ let out a relieved breath.

"I've got you, and I'm not letting go. I'm going to fix you up, okay? It's going to be all right." I was trying to keep it together, but my heart was shredding as she lay in my arms.

"Are you proud of me?" she whispered, as her eyes began to shut again.

I stroked back a blade of her dark brown hair that lay plastered to her cheek. "For what, my love?"

"I stood up to him," she breathed as she closed her eyes, exhausted.

MJ looked at me sharply, and the lanky teenager I had teased, evaporated, replaced by a young man hell bent on protecting his friend. "Kill him," he mouthed to me from the driver's seat, entirely serious.

At one time I thought of Ana's father and myself as one and the same – both monsters, but for different reasons. With her battered body in my arms, I finally understood the truth – Harold Lane and I were nothing alike. More importantly, I was far more dangerous that he could ever be. I met MJ's determined face and nodded.

One of the Lanes was destined to die.

I'd be damned if it was going to be Ana.

44

 ANA

I Jolted Awake, letting out a Strangled gasp when someone kicked me in the shoulder. That's when I realized Kian was holding my arm to my side and MJ was keeping me upright on *Cerberus'* couch.

I swore, but my arm was no longer screaming the way it had been after I ran into my father.

MJ gave my unmarred hand a squeeze as he shifted slightly, leaning me back against the couch. "Easy, Ana. Kian just popped your shoulder back into the socket."

Okay – apparently I wasn't kicked, but it was a heck of a way to get woken up.

I looked around the room and at MJ's strained face and Kian, who was focused on my injuries as the Fallen Marks began to bloom on his face.

I didn't even remember getting to *Cerberus.*

Heck, I didn't remember much of the car ride in general.

Kian looked over to MJ as he tried to slip a hand under the collar of my t-shirt. "I need better access to her skin to heal her properly. I can't get enough contact at the moment."

Finally Kian looked at me, removing his hand from my skin and giving the old t-shirt a tug. "Are you in love with this shirt, Pix?"

I gave a slight shake of my head as I glanced to MJ, feeling awkward. I'd never stripped down to my underwear in front of MJ. Kian, however, had seen a lot more, or rather a lot less, on me.

Kian got to his feet and went to the bar, shuffling around in the drawer, probably looking for scissors. I looked at MJ, who had sat down beside me. "I, uh, didn't realize Dad was home. I guess fate just hates me."

MJ wrapped his warm hand around mine tightly. "This can't continue, Ana. Someday he'll end up killing you, and you know it. The dad you used to have, died a long time ago."

"He was better though. For a while, he was like his old self, you know that," I argued, not wanting to admit that every shred of hope I had for my father, was gone. I was never one to admit something was entirely unsalvageable. He'd been sober for almost three weeks before I ended up living on *Cerberus*. Maybe it was my fault. Maybe he was drinking excessively because I left.

Kian came back over to me, the scissors hanging from his hand, the Fallen Marks covering his skin like an ebony vine. "Pix, MJ's right. It's got to stop. There's no redeeming someone who does this type of damage to their child," he replied sadly, touching my face gently.

"I won't go to the police. I won't." I wasn't about to get flung in the system only a year from freedom. Screw that.

Kian and MJ exchanged a look, and my blood ran cold.

"Don't you dare think you can make him disappear. For god's sake, this isn't some vendetta! I won't have you two involved in some murder conspiracy, MY GOD!" I was getting hysterical and got to my feet, but my head instantly spun.

Kian grabbed me, and pulled me close as he sat me back down. "Okay, Pix. No police and no vendetta. But I need you safe. You deserve to be safe. MJ's right – this can't continue."

Kian brushed his lips softly near my temple and I dragged in a broken breath. "It's okay, Pix. It's going to be okay. We'll figure it out," he whispered against the side of my face.

I lost it completely then, the tears and the ugly sobs causing my aching body to howl more.

Kian kept whispering soothing words to me, but they were all run down by my own bitter gasps. At one point MJ let go of my hand and I heard Kian ask him to give us some space.

In the quiet of the yacht, my sadness began to shrivel, the tears exhausted into nothingness. Part of me was horrifically embarrassed that Kian and MJ had found me in such a state at the junk yard. I felt stripped of my pride and weak.

I hated being weak, or feeling that I wasn't strong enough to push ahead and on my own. I didn't like needing help. Hated it. But my father had pulled out his rage, unfurling it into a vicious onslaught that put me to the ground. I'd finally hit a wall and I knew there was no way I could scale it alone.

"I need help," I whispered to Kian as I traced the black lines on his hand as it rested on my leg. I looked up into his nearly black eyes as he waited, ready to fix the physical hurts and hopefully repair the invisible scars.

"We'll figure it out together, I swear Pix. Maybe we can get you emancipated. Maybe you can be freed from your father's control now, at seventeen, rather than a year from now. You could be a legal adult going into your junior year. You could stay here with me, and he could never force you back to him."

Emancipated?

I never thought about breaking the legal bonds with my father by emancipating myself in the eyes of the law. I could be an adult *now*, free from his rules. He could never force me back to his house if I was free.

I nodded, determined to cut the line that tied me to my father.

Kian kissed me carefully on the lips and then began cutting the t-shirt away from my bruised body. As he exposed my skin, he followed each unwrapped portion with a soft kiss.

I watched, awed, as his Fallen Marks bled onto my own body, following the trail of his lips. As if each broken point on my soul became stained with his love, washing away the hurt and marking me forever with his graceful darkness.

I closed my eyes as the warmth and tingle of his healing took effect, and couldn't help but believe that somewhere, somehow, a greater power had sent me this most unlikely man to become my salvation.

A killer turned savior . . . and my very own fallen angel.

45

KIAN

ANA SPRAWLED HERSELF on *Cerberus'* bow soaking up the sun as I navigated the yacht into the Vineyard Haven Marina – the only dockage we had found that could handle the yacht's size. We'd been here a few times so Ana could work for Waite, but tonight she would attend his estate as a guest and I, as her significant other.

As her boyfriend.

It had only been two days since her birthday. Two days since I found her in the rain, bleeding, and nearly lost my mind. My gift to her had been to heal her and keep her close. To make sure she understood that I was there for her, through anything life threw at her, and that I loved her.

I said it to her a thousand times that night as I held her.

She had cried softly as we laid in bed together, the emotional pain knifing through her until every tear had finally dried up and exhaustion pushed her to sleep. Tucked into my arms, with the blankets curled around her, I knew that we were so much more than a simple label – something that defied both nature and the odds.

I knew with certainty that the myths of being bound to a human and their love equally returned, were not myths. They were truths, spoken by those of my kind who had also found a soul mate in a human. That night, as Ana breathed softly next to me and her heartbeat echoed under her ribs, I knew I'd never love another.

She was my glittering sunrise and my endless midnight, never failing to set my heart racing. And though I'd always see her as that girl who flew under the water on a borrowed surf board, fearlessly pushing herself through the tumbling waves, I also knew she was breakable, hiding a heart that loved even a damaged monster like me . . . and her father.

Healing Pix had run me down, like a human fighting off a virus. I knew I needed to hunt on Sandy Neck to reset my system, so MJ swung by the yacht the following morning. Per his usual, he came loaded with breakfast from Nirvana, but also brought several books on how to become an emancipated minor.

Ana, always one in need of a goal, poured herself into the books. Understanding that she could have control of her life, and the law to back her up, gave her a strength that fired inside her like a comet.

The damaged young woman I'd found the day before had disappeared by the time I'd returned from hunting deer, replaced by the brilliant, defiant siren who had stolen my heart at the beginning of the summer.

She told me she knew what she had to do to be free. She told me her dad would no longer steal her joy. She said we were still going to go to Waite's party, and that I – her boyfriend – would dance with her, which I gladly agreed.

Pix stretched as we neared the docks, her cropped shorts and bikini top making her the epitome of working class hotness. She waved at me, her huge sunglasses swallowing half her face, and then started moving around the boat, readying the tie up ropes for the workers. As I eased *Cerberus* along side its dock, Ana tossed the ropes to the workers who quickly secured our home to the dock.

I cut the engine just as she climbed her way up to my spot on the flydeck, giving me a massive smile. "Nice moves, captain," she said, sliding her glasses on top of her head. Her face was flawless, free from the damage her father had done. "For a second there, I thought you might hit the dock and I was gonna need to take over and show ya how it's done."

"I wasn't paying attention," I replied, hooking my finger into a belt loop on her jeans and towing her against me. "You see, there was this dark haired babe running around the deck and hurling rope at the workers' heads. It was a bit distracting."

I pulled her so tightly against me, that every breath she took pushed against my chest. I loved how alive she felt –

how human. The lurking memory of what her father was capable of tried to weasel into my mind, but I shut it down. Ana was here, with me, and we were going to be free. Both of us.

She brought her face close to mine. "I'm sorry. I didn't know you had a thing for rope hurling," she replied in a whisper against my lips.

"Yeah. I'm trying to cure my addiction. Playboy should dedicate a centerfold to marine knots," I replied, running my hand up her nearly naked back.

"Think I can help you, you know, *not* think about knots? Maybe I can . . . offer myself as an alternative?"

I smiled. "Oh yeah. I think you could even be the cure," I growled, kissing her possessively. She squealed when I lifted her and she clung to me, wrapping her legs around me like a monkey.

I backed her against the controls, but she knocked into the horn and it blared over the harbor, deafening a few of the workers.

She started laughing like crazy as I cursed, trying to move her, only to set off the windshield wipers. Pretty soon she was just a puddle of giggles and snorts as I fumed at the elaborate control panel. "Damn it, next time I'm getting a sailboat. Or a kayak. I mean – what do half of these stupid switches do anyway?"

Ana wiped her eyes as she continued to chuckle. "Really? You drop a boatload of money on *Cerberus* and you don't know what she's capable of? You're crazy."

I sat back in the captain's chair with Ana straddling me. "I'm crazy. Crazy about *you*."

She sighed, calming down and getting serious. A sweet smile appeared on her lips as she tipped forward, giving me a beautiful, simple kiss.

She finally leaned back and ran her fingers across my brow. "Ditto, Key. Ditto."

46

KIAN

WHILE I WAS PLEASED to be escorting Ana to Waite's party, I was equally thrilled to get a chance to possibly snoop around. Thankfully, Waite had invited the public at large, which granted me access to enter his home as a soul thief.

I had a feeling if he knew about my kind, such an act of generosity to the masses would end pretty quickly – nothing like inviting the Darkside in with a free pass to play.

But something was definitely off with our soon-to-be party host, and I doubted he was a pillar of morals to begin with. No one gives money away without expecting something in return, and the last thing Ana needed was another bastard in her life.

And Waite? Total bastard, I was sure.

I stood on the aft deck of *Cerberus*, watching the street lights of Vineyard Haven slowly warm to life as night descended, my mind calculating how to get the most information on Waite over the next few hours.

But then I heard the parlor door slide open, and turned to see Ana appear in the same soft yellow dress I had bought her weeks ago.

She had braided her hair into an elegant concoction that seemed to sweep back and forth on the back of her head, the ends tumbling down her bare shoulders in a riot of soft curls. Somehow she had interwoven the braids with the individual, tiny blue flowers that had been clustered in the vases of the barn room I'd secured for us our first night here.

Back then, nearly two months ago, the night was so similar but it was before I knew the hell she endured. Before the honesty and the kisses. Before I fell entirely in love with her.

She fidgeted with the hem of the short dress, causing it to slide along her smooth thighs. "I, uh, only had this one dress you got me. I never wear this fou frou stuff, but I figured . . ."

"What the hell?" I offered.

She nodded. "Exactly. Do, uh, I look okay? 'Cause I'm worried that if the wind kicks up, I'm gonna flash half the guests."

She continued to nervously bounce and fiddle, which was so unlike her. She was always solid. She knew who she was and was bold enough to give her heart away to me. She was fearless . . . except in a dress, apparently.

I took her hand, stopping her from messing with her outfit. "Do you really have no clue how stunning you look?"

She shook her head, blushing. "No, but you look like a total hottie in your suit, Key. I mean, I think I should carry some pepper spray to ward off the women."

I laughed. "Trust me. I will not be the one needing a bodyguard. Every man at Waite's tonight will be watching you, riveted. You should have pepper spray, but you're going to use it all up on the men that chase you."

I walked over to the bar and pulled open one of the drawers, fetching a small cylinder that had come with the boat. "If you can believe it, the original owner of the boat actually had pepper spray stashed in here. I guess he was a tad paranoid." I handed her the small can of spray.

She smiled, accepting the offering. "I already have pepper spray."

"Really?" I asked, though I shouldn't be surprised. Pix probably carried a few throwing stars and a taser gun as well. But then she tugged my jacket as she rolled her eyes.

"You, ya fool. YOU are my pepper spray. With you beside me, I doubt anyone will come near me. Just don't kill anyone if they ask me to dance." She winced, realizing what she said. "That last part was a, uh, joke by the way."

"Right. No killing anyone. Yes, Ma'am."

She paused, shaking her head as she set the little canister down on a table. "The stuff that comes out of my mouth when I'm with you, is just . .."

"Epic?"

"That's one way to put it," she muttered as I offered her my arm, and we headed into the night to party with a millionaire.

47

ANA

THE WAITE ESTATE WAS more packed than I'd ever seen it before. Several monstrous tents dotted the lawn, and the doors to Waite's art museum were open wide, inviting guests to browse his collection.

Everything was spectacular, including the crystal chandeliers hanging from the tent ceilings, and the tables laden with flowers. Every bush, tree, and entrance was iced with white lights, turning the night into a winter wonderland in the middle of summer.

We found a table near another couple who looked to be in their mid thirties. They were business owners who'd used Mr. Waite's grant foundation to start their own graphic design business on the island. They were lovely and Kian and I kept up a flow of conversation with them over surfboard designs, of all things.

It turned out that they'd been hired by Ripster to design next year's logo, and I asked if they did custom work for boards. When they said they could do just about anything,

I replied that I'd love to see a design of a girl swimming with a shark.

I slid Kian a look when I said it and he smiled broadly. "The shark needs to be pink. Ana loves pink, don't ya sweetie?"

I glared at him, but then he leaned forward and kissed me, whispering a request to dance. I excused us from the couple, and Kian ditched his suit jacket, steering me toward the dance floor at the center of the largest tent.

We joined in with the crowd and bounced and cheered along with them to an awesome Romantics tune, having the time of our lives.

But then the music faded into a sultry jazz mix, and Kian pulled me close and I was reminded of the first time I lost myself in his arms.

It had been here, on the Vineyard, and though it wasn't an elaborate party, I was still wearing this dress. Back then, I felt it – this attraction that nagged relentlessly to be acknowledged.

I ran my hands up and down the silk of Kian's shirt, feeling the strength of his arms and the heat that radiated into my palms. He was watching me, and I studied his face intently, running a finger over his iron jaw.

"You don't look like a monster," I whispered. "How can you be a Mortis? You feel so human – so alive."

His face got serious and he held me a little tighter. "I'm alive, but I'm also suspended in this form. It's as if my timeline was notched the night I was turned, leaving me in a permanent state of twenty-years-old."

I cocked my head, thinking. "I'm glad it happened."

Kian looked shocked.

"No, I mean – I'm sorry it happened to you. I'm sorry someone stole your human life from you and made you . . . this." I rubbed my hand on his chest near his heart. "But I'm also grateful, because if you never became a monster, you would have never been around to become my morally compromised angel."

He smiled broadly, "Excuse me, but I'm not morally compromised."

I snorted. "Oh please – you cop-a-feel more than a Newport socialite in a room full of Prada bags."

Kian slid his hand to the lowest point of my back and across certain round features. "My morals are not compromised if I only want the same stunning, snarky girl every minute of every day. You are my Dr. Frankenstein, Pix. You made the new angel out of the original monster. I'm just hanging on for the ride."

"You're mine, monster or not," I whispered against his lips and then we were kissing as if no one else ever existed. As if time and fate had conspired for centuries to make us fall in love and we would not deny the universe.

At some point I realized someone was clearing his throat behind me. Kian, who had lifted me off my feet, slowly lowered me back to the ground as I looked over my shoulder.

There stood Seth with a model-perfect redhead, her tiny waist easily fitting against him. "You guys may have to pay for the hole you just melted in the dance floor."

I blushed and glanced at Kian, who seemed riveted to the babe with Seth. I mean, yeah – she was INSANELY perfect, but *HELLO?* You're here with your *GIRLFRIEND*.

Kian finally glanced down at me and his face had lost all amusement. His demeanor sent a chill up my back.

Seth looked to his date. "I just wanted you guys to meet Embry. We met a couple days ago at Alchemy. Well, not inside the restaurant, but outside on the street. She is here for the summer."

"I bet she is," muttered Kian and I shot him a horrified glare, mortified by his rudeness. Thankfully Embry seemed unfazed.

I composed myself and shook hands with Embry and introduced Kian and I. "Pleasure," she replied in a cool tone, making me more a fan of Kian's reaction.

"Hey Pix – why don't you show me the garage? I'd love to see that car Seth here had you work on," urged Kian.

"You mean the Electra? Uh, sure," I replied, giving him a questioning eye. I turned back to Embry and Seth, "We'll see you around, guys."

They waved and moved on, but as soon as they'd disappeared into the crowd, Kian hooked me around the waist and quickly steered me toward the garage. I protested most of the way there, demanding answers.

"What the hell was that all about? I've never seen you be that rude to anyone!" I hissed.

Kian shook his head. "That's wasn't just anyone. I bumped into her at Marconi Beach the night I followed you."

"You did WHAT? What are you talking about, *following me?*" I dug my heels in, refusing to move any further until I had answers. Kian and I were relatively alone on the dark expanse of lawn before the massive, 30 car garage.

Kian was tense. "The very first night I met you, you were going surfing. Night surfing, at Marconi. I followed because I knew that most Mortis hunt swimmers at night – it's the best time to pick off someone without getting noticed. I didn't want you to end up dead. I guarded you that night, under the water . . . like a shark."

I swallowed. "You protected me? Back then?"

He nodded. "From the beginning, yes."

"But, why? All I did was fix your car."

Kian took my face in his hands, bringing his eyes down to mine. "Because you were a challenge. You were this fabulously mouthy wisp of a girl, and you fascinated me. I'm grateful, so grateful, I broke down and you showed up to kick my ass. I didn't want anything to happen to you, and watching you surf was like a drug. I became addicted to you that night on the waves."

I stood there, floored.

"But the chick that Seth is with, was there too, and she sure as shit wasn't there to surf. She was there to hunt. She's a soul thief."

"She's one of you? Holy hell, we need to get her away from Seth!" I was having a bit of a freak-out moment and Kian grabbed me by the arms.

"Listen to me, Pix. I'll get her alone and talk to her. Tell her he is a friend and off limits. She should stand down."

My eyes must've been huge like an owl's. "Oh my god – did she kill one of the Howlers? I didn't see anything in the papers about any surf-related deaths from that night."

Kian's brow fell, confusion crossing his face. "Actually . . . you're right. I haven't heard anything about anyone biting the dust either. Why would she have been there, on the beach, except to hunt?"

"Why are you asking me?" I demanded, sharply. "The Howlers have a Facespace page – they'd without doubt post something if someone died. I'm part of that page and so is Seth. I'm sure we would've seen something related to someone dying."

"Wait, wait! You said Seth is part of that page? Is he a Howler as well?" asked Kian, tense.

"Well yeah – he's the one who introduced me to the group. He normally surfs there, but that night he couldn't make it."

"She must've targeted Seth. She targeted him and hasn't killed him yet, which means she needed him for something other than his soul. And she's here . . ." Kian swore. "Shit, she's here for Waite!"

"What? Are you sure?" I asked, dragging Kian towards the back door of the garage that was used by the mechanics. This conversation was getting out of hand.

"Yes. That has to be it. She needed an escort to the party or she would've been out of place, so she used Seth. My kind never wants to draw attention, and she would've, had she been alone."

"We need to find her. NOW," I hissed, pulling open the door to the work bay. I halted in my tracks.

There, in pieces, was a very familiar 1935 Auburn Speedster. Kian froze next to me and I turned to him slowly.

"What's going on? This is the car you – "

Kian quickly covered my mouth with his hand, forcing me back against the wall. I started fighting him, but then he whispered in my ear that our lives were on the line and I needed to play along.

"You never saw me in that car, alright? You never even saw the car, period? I came to your shop and that's how you met me – no Milk Way, no MJ, no Auburn. Do you hear me?" he whispered urgently. "And never tell anyone you saw Embry here, or you could be hunted as a witness."

My eyes grew huge as I began hearing voices somewhere in the garage headed our way. Adrenaline was flying through my body as Kian dropped his hand from my mouth. "Trust me. Please. You've got to trust me."

I nodded and then Kian began kissing me ruthlessly. He pushed his body roughly against mine, running his hand up my thigh, urging the dress upwards. I gasped, about to demand he stop, but then I heard the voices get louder.

"Yeah – it's back here, I think. I – "

The voice halted and Kian broke from me, dropping his hand from my thigh but keeping me pressed against the wall with his body, like a shield. Behind him stood two men in dark jackets and pants. They didn't look like Waite's normal party-goers.

In fact, they looked like bikers. Or gang bangers.

One pointed at us, "Hey you two, get the fuck out. This area is off limits. Go home if you want to pound one another."

Kian, who staggered away from me as if he was a drunk, offered a sloppy smile and slurred apology as he got us out the door. Instantly sober once again, he nearly dragged me from the garage, urging me to keep up with his long, fast strides.

I could barely catch my breath, "What's going on?"

"We need to get back to *Cerberus* and get the hell out of here."

"What about Seth? What about Mr. Waite?" I demanded, but Kian was still pulling me. Finally I yanked my hand free of his and he stopped. "I'm not going anywhere without answers, damn it, and you just about assaulted me against the wall back there!"

"I just saved your life!" he whispered.

"FROM WHO? And why is your friend's car – the car I FIXED – being torn down in the garage?"

Kian rubbed his forehead. "It's not my friend's car. It never was. It belonged to a drug dealer named Sam Benton and I killed him for the Auburn."

I could feel my blood drop to my feet.

Kian stepped forward, but I backed away. "Pix – we need to get out of here. I can explain, but you've got to trust me to keep you safe. That car was loaded with cocaine, but I didn't know it when I first stole it. When I found out, I returned it and Benton's body, but his death never appeared in any papers. It's because Waite's guys went looking for their dope and found Benton and the car. They took both."

"What are you saying?" I asked, truly terrified for the first time in a long time. I started to shiver and Kian reached for me, and this time, I allowed him to pull me to his warm body.

"Waite is a drug dealer. A big player. That's where his wealth comes from. Your father has a loan from a dangerous man. We *need* to get out of here."

I felt like the world fell out from beneath my feet. I thought my life was finally getting better, but it all came crashing down. Kian had killed someone. I fixed a drug car and my father was indebted to a whole different kind of monster.

I worked on the cars that Waite probably used to move drugs – maybe even bodies and god knows what else.

"Oh my god," I breathed, starting to feel sick. My legs felt like they couldn't support me.

Kian pulled me in tighter and forced me to look at him. "It's going to be fine, okay? I can fix it all, but just help me get out of here. Keep it together so we can leave without causing attention, okay?"

I managed a nervous nod and pulled myself together. We needed to get back to the yacht.

48

KIAN

I WAS UNWILLING TO go straight back to Barnstable Harbor on the off chance someone unsavory from Waite's might be waiting for us. I didn't think it would happen, but I chanced nothing with Ana.

She was silent, watching the ocean drift by the yacht as I steered for Newport, a place so wealthy that *Cerberus* would blend (somewhat) with the other million dollar yachts.

I didn't know what to say to Pix. I didn't know how to make all that she had learned seem less . . . horrid. But then she spoke up and shocked the hell out of me.

"With any luck, Embry is there to kill him," she said, never taking her eyes off the night's horizon. "I just don't know *why*. Not knowing why she wanted to get to Waite makes me worried."

I swallowed. "Uh, yeah. That makes me worried as well, but she could just be a hired killer. An assassin, paid by a rival dealer."

Ana turned to me sharply. "Are YOU a hired killer?"

I dared a glance to her and saw a thousand emotions running over her face. "No. I don't take money to kill. You can't hire my murderous side."

She continued to look at me, finally rising to her feet and planting herself on the control dash near me. "But you did kill a man the night you met me?"

I winced. "Yes, I did. I didn't intend to, but he ended up being home and I knew, from my contacts, that he was a drug dealer. He was a scumball and I heard he dealt in everything from heroine to cocaine to pain pills. Trust me – the world won't mourn him."

She sighed, moving over to me, and slipping her arms around my back as she rested her head on my shoulder.

"You're not angry with me?" I asked cautiously.

"Yes. No. I don't know. I watch the news and see all these horrible things happen because of bad people and drugs and guns and . . . and I think you're like Batman, determined to fix Gotham."

"He does have a cool car," I replied, getting hopeful, but she didn't react to my joke.

"Don't kill anyone anymore," she whispered.

"If they try to hurt you, I can't make that promise. And sometimes I need the hit from a human soul. Animals can't sustain me endlessly. But I can promise you, I'll do my best to be Batman and never harm someone who is innocent."

I felt frozen in place with my heart on the line. Instantly I was trying to memorize the feel of her soft body against mine in case she pulled away and left me. I tried to burn her past kisses onto my lips and the sound of her laughter into my mind, terrified this moment was the end. I was fearful that after what I'd revealed, she would no longer be able to see the man under the monster.

I felt her take a deep breath. "Okay," she breathed.

I couldn't believe what she said and I throttled down *Cerberus*, causing the yacht to lean down into the waves.

I turned my head to hers, finding her eyes. "What did you say?"

"I said okay. Kian – no one is perfect. Everyone is messed up on some level, but at least you TRY to do the right thing. Are you a bit of a vigilante? Yes, but it's with honest intent to make the world better."

I went to protest. To correct her, but she was way ahead of me, placing her hand to my lips.

"I know. You probably did some terrible things in your life, Key. Things you regret, deaths that weigh on your conscious. But sometimes we are given a second chance. I'm GIVING you a second chance to be the man I see; a guy who teaches my crazy friend to be a better attack dog, who wears cow print swim trunks and takes orders from a girl when she fixes an engine. I see THAT MAN, and I love him for all his faults and potential."

I turned into Pix and held her tightly, lifting her from the floor so she was higher than me. She ran her hands through my hair and down my face.

"How did I ever deserve you, Ana? I swear to love you to the end of time. Forever and beyond, I will adore you."

She smiled, but rolled her eyes, "Jeez. You soul thieves are such mushy buggers . . ."

I laughed and kissed every inch of her face while she squirmed.

I knew then that everything would be fine. No matter what, we'd be okay as long as we were together.

PART 3

CONSEQUENCES

49

 KIAN

THEY SAY HINDSIGHT IS always 20/20. That if we could see the train wreck coming, we could steer clear of the carnage and all our pain and suffering could be avoided. Some disasters, however, are destined by a higher power and we are forced into the crossfire.

One hour ago, a single phone call unleashed more pain on my beautiful Pixie's life than anyone should ever bear.

God, I'd give anything to turn back the clock and be the one to answer the phone and spare her the agony of finding out her father had suffered a massive heart attack.

I'd sworn to myself that I would protect her, but as the car service drove us from *Cerberus'* dock in Newport to the Boston hospital where he'd been airlifted, I felt as though I'd entirely failed.

She was drowning in her pain, yet all I could offer her was my warmth and my arms and my unfailing love.

I had no idea what we would find once we made it to the ER and the trip through the dark expanse of highway seemed to drag by, slower by the second.

Ana sat tucked against me in the back seat and I kept my arms around her, trying to keep her warm. Her skin was like ice and she repeated the same chant over and over; that her dad would be safe. That he would be all right.

She was in shock, her mind and body failing to communicate the truth of what awaited us. She kept shivering, but she wasn't crying. She wasn't even of sound mind at the moment and I feared that what she would witness in the hospital might shatter her completely.

How breakable she was at the moment was a stark contrast to the girl I knew who was so entirely fearless. She even made me stronger, as was proven out over the handful of hours we had together after Waite's party . . . and before the call.

We had kissed and talked and I finally confessed my history with Mary. I told her that the memory of strangling my fiancé to death was a constant specter in my mind and it kept me guarded, unable to trust myself enough to make love to her.

But Pix believed in me. She believed that the man she saw was not the one who killed Mary, nor was he the monster of childhood nightmares. She had listened to me spill my darkest secrets, finally giving voice to what had happened to a woman who had trusted me, and whose final pleading gasps were engraved on my hands.

Pix had touched me constantly, a simple fleeting contact between two people that conveyed so much. And when she whispered that she wasn't Mary, nor was I a monster, I finally dragged her to me, releasing Mary from my heart. Ana trusted me in the most intimate of acts, and I was finally willing to try.

But we never got there – never made love, for her phone began ringing incessantly. And it wasn't Ana who caved to picking it up . . . it was me. I was the one who held the glowing phone above her as she lay under me, that lazy smile of hers slipping into a frown.

"That's Tim's number, I think," she'd said, drawing her hand from my shoulder and taking the phone from me as I watched her.

Now, as we sat in the car and I tried to quiet her shaking, I replayed the feel of her satin skin beneath me when we were in my bed on *Cerberus.* I remember shifting my weight so I wasn't crushing her, and the rise of her chest pressing to my own as she sighed, finally answering the phone.

And then I felt her breathing stop and her heart begin to hammer . . . and I knew. I just knew.

Nothing good ever comes from a call in the dead of night.

As she listened to the caller, her entire body tightened beneath me, as if someone had slipped a knife silently into her back. I touched her face and asked her what happened, but she was unable to reply and so I eased the phone from her hand, talking to the caller.

It had been one of her father's crew, and through the broken cell connection, I quickly learned of Harold Lane's grave condition and the Coast Guard's fast work of air lifting him to Boston.

I managed to get a car service immediately since the corvette was still parked at the Barnstable docks, and had the presence of mind to call MJ, who vowed to meet us at the hospital with his parents.

"He'll be okay, Kian. He's got to be okay," whispered Ana once again as the hospital's towering exterior appeared through the sedan's window. I felt her weave her hand into my jacket, as if securing herself to me could buy her father a second chance at life.

I pressed a kiss to her forehead as the car slowed in front of the entrance and I saw MJ waiting outside the main lobby door, his back hunched against the cool night air.

If tonight was Harold Lane's last, I begged fate to give his daughter a chance to say goodbye before he left this world.

"I'm here, Pix. It's gonna be okay, I swear," I whispered and I felt her nod as the driver opened our door and MJ finally saw us and ran for our car.

50

 ANA

I COULDN'T UNDERSTAND WHY everyone was just walking about and not racing around, freaking out about my dad. Wasn't this a hospital? Weren't all these people supposed to give a damn about a fisherman whose heart was in trouble?

MJ had pulled me into a bear hug as soon as I stepped from the car with Kian, and he'd led us through the maze of halls to the ER, which was packed with people, none of which were in a panic.

When we finally reached a curtained room, MJ turned to me. "He's in here," he said, but my heart was in overdrive and suddenly I didn't want to see my father, dead on a stretcher.

I slammed on the brakes, trying to catch my breath. "I . . . I don't . . . is he? I can't . . ." I felt Kian's strong hand wrap into mine as my words failed me.

"Is he dead, MJ?" asked Kian and I drew a choked sob as Kian pulled me closer.

"No – no, he's not gone, but he's in bad shape. My parents are here too, Ana. They just went to deal with some paperwork. And your dad's crew is on their way. They were five hours out from Provincetown when the Coast Guard met them, so they have to bring *Charlotte* back in, but they should be here in a few hours."

I swallowed and eased back the curtain and saw my dad lying on the stretcher, a million wires and tubes attached to his body and one larger tube in his mouth. He was sea foam white, and he looked so fragile and cold as death. A bunch of machines whirred and beeped near him, and I felt as though they were ticking off the minutes he may have left.

I forced my feet forward as Kian and MJ hung back, giving me the space I needed for just a moment. Somewhere in the back of my mind I recognized the sound of MJ's mother's voice and that of someone else, probably a doctor.

But I couldn't understand what they were saying as my entire existence was focused on my father, and I carefully placed my hand on the rough white hospital blanket that covered him. I drew my fingers slowly up his still body and over the pattern of the blanket, as if making sure all his limbs were still attached to him.

"Dad?" I finally asked, reaching his head. He looked so breakable, so near death that I was almost afraid to touch his skin. So many devices and wires crisscrossed his body, that I wasn't even sure where was safe to touch, as if my hand on him could cause a catastrophe with the equipment.

Drawing up what little courage I had left, I reached up and touched his eyebrow, smoothing the wiry hair into some semblance of an arch. "Dad? I'm here, okay? You're going to be okay, do you hear me?"

I felt Kian's hand on my shoulder and the sound of something heavy being hauled across the linoleum floor as MJ dragged a chair over for me. I sat down heavily and kept my hand in contact with the bed as I talked softly to my dad.

Over the course of several hours, doctors and nurses were a near constant presence. They'd tell me terms and try to explain things to me, but I didn't fully understand, so MJ's parents stayed with me, trying to decode it all. All I really understood was that my father's heart had stopped, several times, and that he was too weak to be operated on. He was in a coma and he was in bad shape.

His prognosis wasn't good.

Kian and MJ also stayed with me, and at one point the fatigue and stress were so bad, that I nearly passed out and fell from my chair. Kian grabbed me and sat in the corner of the room holding me and I simply lost it, caving to the hopelessness as I sobbed into his shirt.

By morning, the doctors had finally moved my father into his own room and I asked Kian and MJ to give me some time alone with my dad. They did as I asked, and in the silence of the hospital room, I finally gave voice to everything that had happened between us.

I talked about the good times, the rough times, and the truly violent times. I told him all that I felt and how much

I still loved him and forgave him. I told him that, no matter what, I would help him and I'd move back in with him, and everything would be okay.

I also told him that I was afraid.

I was afraid that he wasn't going to make it and that he'd think I hated him because I'd moved out. I was terrified that the last angry words he said to me at Rick's, would be the last that ever passed between us.

I stayed by his side for two whole days, only leaving to eat or briefly sleep against Kian on the stiff sofa by the window that overlooked the streets of Boston.

On the third day, as I spoke to Dad quietly, I started to hear one of the machines beep louder and I thought for one fleeting moment he was waking up. That he would open his eyes and tell me he was going to be okay.

But it wasn't that kind of beep, and soon all the alarms were going off. The door to his room burst open and doctors and nurses pushed me aside and began a coordinated, high-speed dance around my father, grabbing things and stripping the sheets from his body.

That's when I realized that death was a very probable outcome of the next few minutes.

I became frantic. Started yelling at people to help him just as Kian and MJ raced back into the room, and suddenly hope bloomed brilliantly inside me.

I could defy Death with the help of the one man who said he would never fail me. Who said he would always be there for me.

I ran to Kian, grabbing him by the arms, and pleaded for him to save the one man he truly hated. Begging him to restore my father's broken heart.

Kian refused.

51

IT HAD BEEN NEARLY A YEAR since I'd lost my father to a failing heart, and Kian to my own grief and rage.

Last summer, before it all went so terribly wrong, Key and I had been in love. Back then we fit each other, both missing our own pieces that could only be filled by one another. And back then, he'd been right, even about the ferry: it did smell like mold and tourists. But to me, it also smelled like coffee and diesel and ocean. It reminded me of the men I'd loved and lost and how it smelled like home.

A home that now felt . . . empty.

Sitting across from MJ as he dug through a Cracker Jack box for his promised prize, I was hit with a fierce case of *Kian*.

That's what I called it – those moments when something simple brought the memories of him rushing back to me so hard, I thought my heart would stop.

Sometimes it came out of nowhere – a vicious hit and run to my soul. Over the past eleven months, I learned to deal with those moments by drawing from my anger; my sense of absolute betrayal. But the anger was starting to fade, replaced simply by the pain.

The hours following Waite's party had been the most unforgettable and devastating of my life. That night, it was Kian who told me I should take the call. Honestly, I had no intention of answering it, and some days, I wish I never had.

Some days I wish that fate had taken him – my father – quickly and decisively at sea.

I think back to that night often, though I try my best not to. But here, on the ferry with MJ and headed to Martha's Vineyard for a surfboard rally, everything reminded me of Kian.

Everything reminded me of what I had with him, and all that I lost in a matter of hours.

That night, after we'd left Waite's party and docked in Newport, Kian confessed what he'd done to Mary. About the guilt and the fear he carried and how it held him back.

I remember how I kissed him and undressed him and convinced him that he was no longer that monster, and that I'd never be Mary. He said that what we shared was unlike anything he had ever felt before, and that he'd heard other soul thieves speak of a supernatural link between his kind and humans.

He'd always thought it was just a myth . . . until me.

I understood exactly what he was saying, for my love for him reached past anything I'd ever known before or even thought was possible. And in that moment, I was ready and he was finally willing, but we never finished what we started because my phone rang.

It rang over and over, and when I finally answered it, my perfect summer turned brutally cruel.

I can still feel the phone resting against my ear as Tim told me that my father had suffered a massive heart attack, the metal and glass feeling hot against my cheek. I felt as though I'd lost contact with reality – as if I was stuck in a hellish dream that I couldn't shake myself from.

But it wasn't a dream and by the time we made it to Boston, my father was on life support. His heart had stopped several times and he was in a coma.

I remember holding his roughened hand, begging him to stay. Promising him I would come home and that we could work on getting him better. I promised him my unfailing love and that I wouldn't leave him like my mom had.

I remembered screaming at people to help him. To fix him . . . and that's when I looked to Kian. I begged him to save him. Tried convincing him that Dad was actually a good guy and he just needed help. I reminded Key that he'd sworn he would never break my heart.

I told him that if he truly loved me, then he would heal my father, but he refused. He told me some horrible lie about how he couldn't save someone whose heart had already stopped. He said that my father would end up like him – a Mortis – and that he would be violent as a soul thief.

I told him I didn't care and that he could teach my dad how to live peacefully.

Kian said no.

I remember hitting him and MJ trying to pull me off. I screamed at Key, calling him a murderer and a liar. I flailed, accusing him of just playing with me, of never truly loving me, and that I never wanted to see him again as long as I lived.

Now, however, with so many months between that night and today, my anger was still raw, but my heart would trip whenever I saw a stunning yacht. None ever had a ruby hull. None were *Cerberus*.

It didn't matter. Kian would never recognize me now anyway. I had razored off most of my brown hair, down to a boy cut and bleached of color.

My life consisted of RC Garage, MJ, and Dalca. That was it. I rarely surfed anymore, and only agreed to come to the Vineyard because MJ had nagged the piss out of me.

Junior year – a year that was supposed to be spent living with Kian, finding myself and my freedom, and maybe even making a few new friends – instead crawled by in loneliness and the plain white walls of my studio apartment above the shop. I expected more of the same when senior year began in a month.

On the worst nights, a dark voice would whisper temptations in my head of how I could end the agony. On those nights, I'd drag the yellow sundress out of its worn Vineyard Vines bag and hold it tight to my chest as I slept.

I pretended it smelled like him and that his hands still swept over the fabric as he kissed me and slept beside me.

"Hey. Where you at, girl?" asked MJ, watching me, concern etched on his face.

I forced a smile. "I'm right here, weirdo, watching you stuff yourself in pursuit of a plastic toy."

Hiding my pain from MJ was the hardest, like wearing chainmail every minute of every day. He knew me the best, could peel me apart and force a confession if he wanted to.

But as he looked at me, he seemed to know he couldn't push the issue today. Seemed to know I was too close to shattering.

He smiled back at me, but it didn't reach his eyes as he held up a tiny compass speckled with popcorn bits. "Want my toy? It points to true north – pretty cool, for a Cracker Jack prize."

I held out my hand and he placed the small device in my palm. "Thanks, MJ."

"Anytime, Ana. I think it's better suited to you anyway," he replied.

"Because I'm awful with a map?"

"No," he replied, his smile falling. "Because you look, for once, lost."

52

THE LAST TIME I saw Ana Lane, she was shrouded in black.

During her father's funeral, I'd hidden myself a few hundred yards away, tucked against a cluster of spruce trees at the cemetery. She had stood alongside MJ and his parents, along with an older woman and a handful of men who I assumed were her father's shipmates.

She was officially an orphan, abandoned by her mother and betrayed by her father . . . and me. The sound of her broken goodbyes drifitng over the green lawn, cut through me like a jagged knife.

The sight of her kneeling to kiss his casket will haunt me forever.

I wanted to be there, next to her, comforting her, but I was responsible for his death. I played God, and sacrificed one Lane to save the other.

She had begged me to fix him – to heal his damaged heart. And quite honestly, I may have attempted it had it not been for MJ.

When we had arrived at the hospital, MJ was already there with his parents, and Ana ran straight for her father in the emergency room. MJ, however, yanked me aside and towed me into an alcove with a pay phone. He knew, already, what I was fearing: Ana would look to me for help.

She would seek my ability to rescue the one man I was trying to save her from.

MJ had been forceful as he spoke, determined to keep Ana from her father. *"If you fix him, you'll have signed her death sentence. You saw the results of two nights of his anger, but I've seen years! I've found her unconscious in her room, found her so badly beaten that she couldn't stand. He will kill her and it's only a matter of time. If you ever really loved her – if you are really as selfless as she says you are – you'll let him die."*

I knew MJ was right. I knew if Harold Lane lived, his daughter would be by his side, trying to get him well. She would live in the lion's den until he slammed her head against a sharp corner, ending her life. I also knew that to let Harold die, was to destroy Ana in a whole different way . . . and our relationship would never survive. She would see me as the selfish killer I was designed to be.

Yes, I could save him, but Harold would never be human again. He would end up like me, a killer, only more unforgiving. A stopped heart, restarted by a soul thief, was how our kind was born – how we became infected and our own soul, destroyed. We were a chance to cheat death, but at a staggering cost.

Ana's father's heart was failing fast. It had stopped numerous times, only to be restarted by the doctors. If I shared my ability with him, the beast he was as a man would be amplified as a monster.

Telling her *no* when she begged me was the most selfless thing I'd ever done in my existence. It was also the most devastating. She called me a murderer. Banished me from her life until the day she was "rotting in her own grave."

I left her as she asked, but only after MJ assured me he'd keep her safe and watch out for her. He also agreed to make sure that he'd contact me if Ana ever needed anything – if she ever needed me.

I never heard from him again.

No day ever passed without thinking of her and how profoundly she changed me. Yes, I hunted humans, but I now leaned towards using Blacklisted people, bought from the Dealers. I continued to live on *Cerberus*, having brought her down to various southern ports, until I ended up here, in Miami . . . and looking at a very familiar guy playing pool.

I'd entered the bar simply to take a look around and see if my Blacklist target was inside, but instead I came face to face with a blatant reminder of Cape Cod, Elizabeth, and every other memory I tried to bury: Raef Paris.

He was taking aim on a complex combination shot when I dropped a pool cue onto the felt table.

He looked up at me, an eyebrow raised. "Ah. I should've known. If there's a rude jackass within a ten mile radius of this place, it HAS to be you. How does the self-obsessed life go, Kian?"

I started pulling the balls from the pockets and tossing them onto the table, mainly to piss him off and mess with his game. Raef and I always clashed because I thought of him as beneath me – especially when we were still human.

Tonight, however, I wanted to hang out with a piece of Cape Cod, even if it was Raef. I was pretty desperate, obviously.

Though he'd been a blue collared carpenter back in our human days, Raef had since built his wealth. Immortality made retirement a moot point, and placing one's money in the right places made it grow exponentially.

We were basically on the same footing with regards to money now, but Raef still acted like the quiet carpenter he was when he was turned at eighteen. Together, we made an interesting contrast.

He leaned back against the wall as I racked the balls. "I'm assuming you'd like to play a round?" he asked, watching me work.

"Maybe just a few. What shall we bet?" I asked, offering him the first shot.

"I don't gamble, Kian. Plus, there's nothing I really want badly enough to duel over. I doubt there's a single thing on this planet that's out of your deep-pocketed reach."

"There are some things money can't buy, Raef. Trust me."

Raef gave me a curious look. "Did the great Kian O'Reilly actually come up against something he couldn't obtain? The world must be coming to an end."

"Maybe," I replied, and a vision of my beautiful Pix drifted through my mind. "Definitely."

If fate had a shred of mercy, I would someday see Ana Lane again . . . and win this one game against Raef Paris.

Ana and Kian's story continues in UNDERTOW.

True love never dies.

Never.

Are you in need of help?

Are you fearful for your safety?

You are not alone.

The National Domestic Violence Hotline is available 24/7 by calling 1-800-799-7233 or going to their website at http://www.thehotline.org

⤶ ACKNOWLEDGEMENTS ⤷

I can never thank all of the people who've always pulled for this series – there are so many, and I'm truly humbled by their endless cheering. Without doubt, Cruel Summer was written for the fans, who begged me for the story of how Kian and Ana met. This book is 100% for them.

A huge thanks, as always, to my mother for her devotion to my pursuit of the story, and to the rest of my family for pulling together to give me time to write. A big thank you to my daughter, Kalli, who is the most organized teenager ever and who managed to keep my office in great shape (despite my chaotic ways).

CRUEL SUMMER ~ K.R. CONWAY

Massive thanks to my Beta team, including Charlotte, Sabine, Layla, Kat, Bethany, and Lindsey. They see the characters as real people and demand greatness from them . . . and from me. Actually, I basically live in fear of failing my Beta team because I suspect they stocked weapons and poisons if I fail. Nothing says motivation like a few well-formulated threats.

Huge thanks to Justin Blaze and Christa Mullaly who were the original models for Kian and Ana, and Sean Potter who became the face of MJ. Their photos can be found throughout the Internet as their characters, and I continue to use their amazing camera-ready faces for much of our book swag. They believed in the characters and brought them to life, often directing themselves in front of the camera. The picture of Justin (Kian) alongside Christa (Ana) was entirely their doing, and if Sean could shift into a black dog, I'm pretty sure he would. In fact, MJ's penchant for metal music came directly from Sean. Also, a big thanks to Alex Daunais for his great skills behind the lens.

As always, a big thank you to Cape Cod and the places that spark my imagination daily: Barnstable Harbor

(Hyannis, MA), The Boarding House (Hyannis, MA), The Flying Horses (Martha's Vineyard, MA), The Lavender Moon (formerly of Sandwich, MA), The Steamship Authority (Woods Hole, MA), Vineyard Vines (Martha's Vineyard, MA), The Hot Chocolate Sparrow (Orleans, MA), Nirvana Coffee Shop (Barnstable, MA), Heritage Museum and Gardens (Sandwich, MA), Craigville Pizza and Mexican (Centerville, MA), The Wellfleet Drive-In (Wellfleet, MA), and of course, Four Seas Ice Cream (Centerville, MA).

Come to Cape Cod, visit our world, and live the Undertow series for yourself . . .

⤳ ABOUT THE AUTHOR ⤳

Twitter: @sharkprose

Instagram: k_r_conway

Facebook: KR-Conway

Young Adult novelist K.R. Conway, has been a professional journalist since 1999. She is also an editor, graphic designer, and critique partner for other writers. She was named "Writer in Residence" of the award winning Sturgis West high school in Massachusetts in 2014, and is a member of the SCBWI.

Her debut novels *Undertow* and *Stormfront* frequent the Amazon bestseller lists and were added to high school summer reading lists and teen book clubs. The series has spawned fan fiction, won top-pick awards from reviewers and librarians, and drawn reluctant readers into a twisted tale of murder and mayhem set on Cape Cod.

Conway, who holds a BA in dangerous weirdos (forensic psych) from Mount Holyoke College, also drives a 16-ton school bus filled with her iPod-toting target audience simply because she likes the torture. She lives on Cape Cod with two opinionated kids, a fishing-obsessed husband, and an assortment of mismatched pets.

Her website offers a peek into her twisted psyche:
http://www.capecodscribe.com

21605390R00187

Made in the USA
Middletown, DE
05 July 2015